PHOENIX DAWN

AND THE RISE OF THE WITCH

TO ELLEN,
ENJOY, MISS
YOU!

ET

To ELLEN,
ENJOY, WIZZ
YOU!

PHOENIX DAWN

AND THE RISE OF THE WITCH

BY

APIXAL

ILLUSTRATIONS BY GARETH DAVIES

ERIC TROWBRIDGE
JOSH WALKER
HAYLEY RUIZ
JOSE RUIZ

Edited by Audrey van Ryn.

Library of Congress Control Number: 2015911807

ISBN-13: 978-0-9963010-7-7
ISBN-10: 0-996-30107-0

Printed in the U.S.A
First edition, August 2015

www.apixal.com

The dedication of this book belongs to all of our wonderful Kickstarter supporters for whom without this would not be possible. As well to all of the apixal family members and friends who believed in us from the very beginning.
We are forever grateful.

The journey through Mythe continues
in our forthcoming game based on this book.

Join our community and stay in touch.

apixal.com
facebook.com/apixal
twitter.com/apixal
instagram.com/apixalgames

PREFACE

What an incredible journey this has already been. On my birthday in June 2014, I left my job at Apple Inc. after eight years. The passing of Steve Jobs was a sign for me to find my own path. Steve often spoke of how important it was to live a life without regrets. What would I regret if I were told I only had months to live? If you truly ask yourself this question, you will realize that it is not the things you did that you regret, it's the things you didn't do: spend more time with your family, travel more, and for me starting my own company.

Apixal was born shortly after my departure from Apple in June of 2014. I started the company with hopes of creating a wonderful world where we could build video games, novels, and other types of entertainment that would be fun and unique. This book is the first labor of love and I hope it lives up to that mark.

This book is broken into three acts, each act telling and continuing the story from the perspective of different characters. The third and final act of this book is our upcoming game's complete storyline. The game will be a role-playing adventure allowing you to explore Mythe and battle the mythical creatures you're about to meet. I believe that one of the key aspects in creating a great role-playing game is a great story. Knowing that, we felt spending the time to write this novel would be a superb long-term investment that we could use as a solid foundation for our game.

This book is nine months worth of work. I couldn't have done it without the wonderful team here at apixal. Their energy and passion behind Phoenix Dawn continue to make this the best job in the world. Now, sit back, relax and enjoy.

Eric Trowbridge
Founder of apixal

CONTENTS

PHOENIX DAWN

AND THE RISE OF THE WITCH

....

He extends one of his arms and opens his palm, revealing a misshapen piece of scrap metal and saying, "I made this ring for you."

I lift the ring with caution and examine all the sharp edges, knowing I would lose a finger if I ever attempted to wear it.

"Thank you AP-12, it's beautiful." I say, smiling and appreciating the gesture.

He chuckles, proud of his accomplishment. Each day, AP-12 offers me one of his mangled creations. I can never tell what they are, but I keep each one on display in my room.

....

ACT ONE
THE MOTHER

CHAPTER ONE
AWAKENING

They took us, carrying, my brother and I away into the dark night. There was a train. I watched the world being destroyed from the window near my seat. Fires, anarchy, people fighting to survive in an Earth different than the one I knew growing up. All of us silent on our way to our unknown destination. Now I am here.

Forgotten, am I forgotten? It seems that way sometimes, especially when the sun goes down and the lights go out. Only six months ago we were normal people living normal lives. Now we are beyond menial accomplishments, but we yearn to return to the mundane.

Below me, Zuri snores, inhaling slow deep breaths and releasing them in rhythm. The sound echoes in our small room. Even if I wanted to sleep – which I don't – I wouldn't be able to. Her life's ambition was to retire young and travel the world... She never made it further than Fifth and Main.

Careful not to disturb her, I throw off my thin, worn blanket and roll out of my top bunk, landing like a cat on the pads of my feet and hands. I stretch. My joints feel stiffer than usual. She remains undisturbed, her long black hair covering her pillow. Standing up, I turn and leave the room.

Technological advances in recent years have forced people to take sides, either adopting the technology or fighting to stifle its growth. Wars are nothing new, though. That is how humanity has always been.

This early morning is different than others. The evidence comes in the form of a soft hum in the air, a sound I've never heard before and one that many people might not notice.

The cold beneath my bare feet reminds me I am still alive as I creep through the dark, knowing it will still be a few minutes before the lights turn back on. I prefer the dimness. It allows me to imagine my surroundings as I'd like them to be and not as they are: plate glass windows and solid white walls. Two levels of twenty rooms are placed around a communal area in the middle of the ward. Each room is a thick piece of glass, making us feel more like animals in a sterile lab than prisoners.

I say the room is a ward, but it is really a circular shape, rails and narrow walkways on the second level with a single, spiral staircase going up. Walls, ceiling, and floor alike are all painted white: bright, specular, and clean. Not that long ago every room was full. Only five of us are left now: the others dead, driven mad, or dragged away for some experiment, never to be seen again. Olivia was taken just yesterday.

My fellow survivors sleep, conjuring up happy dreams of a not so distant past and finding solace in those memories. Remembrances are the only motive for us to keep going.

I pass by my twin brother's room, glancing in as I walk by. His name is Doug. Since our arrival he has been through the most, dying three times during experiments. Stubborn as my brother and I are, he refused to stay dead. It is how he earned his nickname — Lazarus. I can't imagine facing this place without him.

His frame is tall and muscular. He has dusty brown hair and piercing, intelligent blue eyes. Like most twins, Lazarus and I have always been close.

He rolls back and forth in his bed, moaning and mumbling. His words are nonsense, something about Ais and Apollyon. I've asked him what those words mean and each time he replies, "It is better not to know some things".

If not for Lazarus I'm not sure I'd have been able to manage my first weeks here. Casting my gaze back to him, I sigh, turn, and continue on.

Metal clanks overhead as the air purification and heating turn on. I look up...not that I can see the strange contraption in the dark: a large, white box with vents positioned over the communal area. I'm not entirely convinced it ever worked. Even if it did, I'd give just about anything to inhale a breath of fresh, unfiltered air and feel the warmth of the sun on my skin.

I pass empty chamber after empty chamber on the way to the next occupied room. Poking my head inside, I see the youngest of us, physically no older than eight or nine years. Intellectually, he may be the most mature of us. His name is Habbicus but we call him by his last name, Twigs. He is unhealthily thin and pale. Under his covers I can tell his knees are bent, his arms hugging them against his chest. His hair is blond and messy. A book titled The King in Yellow lies on the floor by his bed. The strange thing about the book is it doesn't have the library mark associated with the other books from the facility, making me wonder how Twigs got it. Most kids his age read simple, thinner books. But if he were normal, if any of us were, they wouldn't have kidnapped us. As I pull my head out of the room I see him moan and shiver again.

A faint, barely audible chatter can be heard in an adjacent area of the ward. It means the robotic guards and scientists will be here soon. Will we all make it through the day or will I wake up with one fewer friend tomorrow? Maybe my friends will wake up without me. We are always afraid but what choice do we have but to live with the fear?

Moving to the stairway, I stop when I hear a scuffling behind me. Pivoting to look back, I see AP-12. His head and body are painted the same white as the ward walls. Emotionless eyes are reminiscent of binoculars, ending in big, round, black lenses. He moves by rolling on eight wheels, four on each side. His arms seem almost human, insulated and reinforced to lift and move the heaviest of objects with ease. His hands come complete with opposable thumbs. As I look at him he stops, extending his cylindrical body up so that he's eye to eye with me. With an inquisitive, albeit robotic intonation, he asks me, "Why are you up so early? Are you not tired?"

"I'm not tired," I insist, and smile.

A sequence of bleeps is emitted. I've always interpreted this sound as laughter. "Of course not. Who needs sleep?"

"Not you and me," I answer, patting him on his head. "So, AP-12, what have you made me today?"

He extends one of his arms and opens his palm, revealing a misshapen piece of scrap metal and saying, "I made this ring for you".

I lift the ring with caution and examine all the sharp edges, knowing I would lose a finger if I ever attempted to wear it.

"Thank you, AP-12, it's beautiful," I say, smiling and appreciating the gesture.

He chuckles, proud of his accomplishment. Each day, AP-12 offers me one of his mangled creations. I can never tell what they are, but I keep each one on display in my room.

I move up to the second level of our ward. AP-12 remains below, though he's more than capable of maneuvering his way up the steps. "Have a nice day," I hear him say. Then I hear his wheels carrying him in the other direction.

Following the circular railway, I reach the room which the fourth and final prisoner inhabits. We call him Enkidu. He has been here the longest of all of us. In his pre-captive life he was CEO and founder of a major tech company.

Around fifty years old, he is a man with a full head of dirty blond hair. He's of short stature, with a stocky build, square face, and a round nose. He chooses to be on the top floor because, as he puts it, he feels "more comfortable up there, away from people". I suppose not being on the same level as the rest of us and having a higher vantage point gives him some peace of mind.

Climbing the steps, I round the bend and reach Enkidu. On a top bunk he sleeps – one eye open and one shut, his arms crossed over his chest – his thick glasses hanging from the bed frame next to him. I'm not sure how he taught himself to sleep with an eye open, or how the eye tracks me as I move into the doorway. It doesn't really matter. What does matter is that all of us are still here and still alive. Not sure if he's awake, I wait a few seconds for a response. When none comes, I begin to step away.

"Taking an early morning walk?" Enkidu startles me when he speaks.

"Yes, Enkidu." I smile, turning to him.

"You shouldn't worry about me or anyone else, Amy." I see him putting on his glasses and sitting up in bed. "This is a dangerous place and worrying about others is a good way to get yourself into hot water. Don't assume any of us will care the same way for you."

"This place isn't one where a person can survive all alone. It'll drive them mad… Don't take this the wrong way, but it seems like you are halfway cracked, already." I wink.

"Only halfway? I've been taking a ride on the crazy train for some time, now. I'd be certifiable…if I weren't already locked up." His eyes squint. "Hmm, what do you want?"

I reply, "Well, the scientists have been talking. They don't think I can hear them, that I'm too distracted with the tasks we've been given. They say something big is about to happen, a final test. You know what that means?"

He responds, "It means Lazarus is in for long weeks of poking and prodding."

"He'll be okay. He's my brother. We are a lot alike, you know," I insist, trying to sound hopeful. My brother is everything to me.

"Let me offer you some fatherly advice. The day will come where none of us will be okay. Remember to never fully depend on others, those who will only let you down." Enkidu removes his blanket, swings his legs over the edge of his bed, and stretches with a yawn. "Time to wake up," he says and hops down. As his feet touch the ground the artificial lighting flickers on throughout the entire facility. "I hope breakfast is something other than mush of oats," he snarls. Mush of oats is the nickname we've given to the food we are served. The scientists call it something else, a long fancy word which is not worth remembering.

We step out of the room and observe the single doorway into our ward. It has lights above it which flash yellow twice, accompanied by corresponding beeps as the locks over the door snap, clanking open. Two black-clad, armed robot guards funnel through the entryway, positioning themselves on each side of the opening. These guards physically appear to be human. However, they lack the emotional intelligence and humanistic tendencies of AP-12.

On a normal day it would be the science team which followed but today it is different. A woman named Prefect Gray crosses the threshold, her dress suit tight on her short round body... Each time we see her she seems a bit rounder. Her hair is bleach blonde, pulled back into a tight bun. Dark red lipstick is liberally applied and she uses a lighter shade of makeup. She walks into the center of the communal area and stops, wearing a forced smile. A simple white table with stools is next to her. There used to be more of them but as people disappeared so did the tables. I whisper to Enkidu, "It is obvious she's been eating more than mush of oats". He smiles.

Still standing, she begins. "So happy to see you all once again. I presume you're doing well?" She pauses, as if waiting for an answer. When none comes she continues as if we had. "Good, good, now let us move on to why I am here. Today we will be beginning the final phase of your evaluations.

"As is customary, we will be having a new team of scientists working with you as we move into this phase."

Leaning on the rail, Enkidu and I watch. Enkidu's theory is that Prefect Gray is protecting some hidden secret by limiting information between groups.

Prefect Gray finishes, "I'm happy to introduce Dr. Avi Taylor, the head of the new team".

A young man in a white lab coat enters the room and stands next to her. He's tall, with smooth black hair and a goatee. "Hello, everybody," he says. "I am happy to meet you all. As Prefect Gray said, my name is Dr. Avi Taylor but you can just call me Avi."

"Go away," Twigs declares. His voice carries through the open space, making it easy to understand the calm assertiveness in his tone.

"Yeah, go away," Enkidu repeats with a whisper, and giggles.

"Shh..." I order, focusing my attention on the new scientist. Call it a woman's intuition but something seems different about him: his expression, gestures, the tone of his voice. I don't know how he's different but it makes me uneasy.

Avi fixates on Twigs, maintaining a calm voice. "Why do you say that?"

Without missing a beat, Twigs answers, "Because I don't want you here. None of us do. I'm not going to pretend to be happy in a place where I feel a prisoner, nor will I be bitter. I am a realist."

"Here come the big words." Enkidu rolls his eyes.

"All of my life I have been ostracized as if I were some strange contagion."

Enkidu whispers, "What nine-year-old says 'ostracized'?"

"Shhh..." I repeat, glaring over at Enkidu.

"Yes, ma'am!" he says, and salutes.

I roll my eyes, shake my head, and return my attention to Avi and Twigs.

Twigs continues, stepping closer to Avi and away from his room. "They needed to feel like they were better than me. People are like that and in the end it doesn't matter if it is an individual or a group of people. Our world makes us suffer so they can live. Once they have what they want we will be swept under the rug, the saviors who history forgot. I don't like anyone who uses me. Your whole organization stands for the abuse and oppression of innocent people, of me and my companions here. I'd rather you go away." There is a strange apathy in his words, no emotion, just a calm insistence.

Tension builds, an uneasy anxiety inside of me. I've never been good with conflict. Growing up, I never had to be. When I saw contention I would avoid it: pretending not to notice it, distancing myself from its source, and hoping it would pass. Too bad none of those is an option at the moment.

Unblinking, Avi listens and waits for Twigs to finish. Looking at Twigs eye to eye and speaking with a calm voice, he says, "Are you done?"

"For now," Twigs smiles.

Avi waits, his eyes focused with an intensity, watching Twigs for a few more seconds. Then his expression softens and he turns his attention back to us.

"I want to invite you all to the library today. I have some questions about your files and would like to see how your abilities are progressing. When it is not your turn for testing, you will be allowed R&R. Feel free to check out as many books as you would like from the library. This phase of testing, from what I understand, will be much less taxing on you than the previous phases."

"Less taxing? You sound like a politician," Enkidu shouts.

The joke is so corny I can't help but laugh.

Lazarus shakes his head in amusement.

Enkidu chimes, "I thought it was funny".

Avi continues, "Well, it was nice to meet you all". He casts his eyes up at me, holding me in his gaze for a few seconds and creating an uncomfortable moment. It makes me afraid but I'm not sure of what. I watch as he turns. His white lab coat billows behind him as he follows Prefect Gray out of the room.

After the door shuts I begin the walk down the steps to meet the others. Enkidu, planning to remain upstairs for the time being, stops me. He is comfortable with speaking to people in public settings, but on an interpersonal level, I've never heard him speak with anyone other than me. "You know what is funny?" he says, interrupting my germinating thoughts about our new lead scientist.

"What is that?" I ask.

"We are always testing limits, but I have a feeling it will be this place which pushes Avi to the edge — not us. A new day dawns, and for the first time in a long while, I think this one brings with it some light."

Mush of oats isn't as bad as it sounds. It is much, much worse: a slimy liquid resembling oatmeal, with a stale cardboard flavor. Prefect Gray insists it is enough to nourish a strong physical body and support the physiology of the mind. What I wouldn't give for a slice of pizza.

Two guards stand by as we eat, Lazarus and me on one side of the table, Zuri and Twigs on the other. Enkidu sits on the floor with his back against the wall, as far away from everyone as the guards allow. If they let him eat in his room I'm sure he would.

I hear the familiar beeping of AP-12 behind me. He tends to avoid the guards when they are in the ward. I see him in the corner emptying the trash, collecting random bits, no doubt for tomorrow's gift.

Four windows are evenly spaced in the ceiling; they open each morning, letting in natural light. Today for some reason they don't, adding to my growing sense of impending doom. I want to believe what Prefect Gray and Avi tell us, that we aren't trapped and hopeless.

Twigs chimes in and breaks the silence. "They'll never let us leave. What I said to the new scientist is true. People are selfish. Taking advantage of us, these people are no different. Once they have what they want, they can't risk letting us leave. To keep us in line they'll pretend to be our friends and tell us pretty things."

Feeling the need to provide some counsel, I tell him, "You're far too young to be so cynical, Twigs. If you keep it up you'll be giving Enkidu a run for his money." I glance over at Enkidu and he's staring back, like he knows I'm talking about him. Smiling, he waves, and I continue, returning my attention to Twigs. "The whole purpose of life is to bond with other people. Even humanity's earliest ancestors depended on each other to survive in a harsh world. We have always been stronger in teams."

Twigs replies, "The funny thing about teams is that they always have a coach, someone to order them around: Avi, Prefect Gray, these guards, and the other scientists. They are coaches. If we are going to survive this we need to become coaches, the ones in control. For us to gain that control we need to understand our purpose in this place. Lazarus tells you things will be fine. He's the one who should know that isn't the case...or maybe he'd care to answer your questions about Ais and Apollyon?"

Lazarus deflects. "Twigs, do you know the story of Pandora's box?"

Twigs nods, declaring, "Of course I do. Pandora unleashed all of the evil on the world because of her curiosity. The last thing in the box was Elpis, the spirit of hope."

"Right. It is important we hold on to Elpis so we can overcome the other evils we face."

"Hope won't save us. Resourcefulness will...and resilience," Twigs grunts.

The door to the ward slides open and Avi steps through, accompanied by two new guards and holding a clipboard in his hand. These two guards are different than any I've ever seen before, dressed in white instead of the traditional blue. They seem to be human. I've never seen human guards here before. Avi flips through some papers, examining them, and then glances up at us. "Mmm...I see you are all still eating. Please, take your time. As soon as you are done I'd like to evaluate you one at a time."

"I'm ready to go with you, now," Twigs volunteers. "I don't have much of an appetite." He stands up and walks over to Avi.

Avi doesn't allow the tone of his voice or expression to fluctuate. "Habbicus it is. I'll be back for the rest of you later." He turns and leaves the room, Twigs and the guards following. The door shuts behind them.

"I'm worried about Twigs," I confess to the others.

"Bah, he's still a kid," Zuri interjects. "He'll grow out of it."

"I hope so." I explain, "I think I'm so concerned for him because he reminds me so much of our own family. Lazarus and I have two little brothers. The thought of them being alone in a place like this would be terrifying to me. Twigs probably has someone out there who is wondering about him, an older sister or mother. We owe it to them to take care of him."

"You're right," Zuri agrees, adding, "It is good for you to watch out for him."

Lazarus takes a bite of his breakfast. "I'm sure Twigs will appreciate what you are doing for him." He stirs his mush of oats. "Do you think his parents were anything like ours?"

"I have never heard you talk about your parents before. What were they like?" Zuri asks.

"Fun," Lazarus and I say together. I add, "Life was never boring in our home. I remember music was important to them, so they enrolled us in piano lessons when we were very young, eight or nine years old. Using that as a base, I learned the violin, flute, and guitar. Lazarus wanted to be a Ninja Turtle so they put him in karate."

"You played the guitar? I did too!" Zuri pronounces, pride and excitement easily recognized in her voice. "I wish we had some guitars here. It would give us something else to do aside from reading books all day long. Why didn't you tell me you played guitar before?"

"It never came up before."

"Ah! A likely story," she retorts, letting a hint of skepticism and a large dose of humor sneak into her voice.

Lazarus adds to my memories of our childhood. "When we weren't at home, we were either at church or school. If we weren't there, we were at a creek not far from our home." I twirl my hair, listening to Lazarus and reminiscing about the past. "Of course, I took every opportunity to throw my sister into it when she wasn't looking." He laughs and squeezes my shoulder.

I add, "So many good times before we were taken".

A brief moment of silence overcomes us at the mention of being taken. Zuri has been slow to share details of her past and whenever we talk about how we were kidnapped, her eyes seem to avoid contact.

Glancing over at Enkidu, I wonder aloud, "How do you think they caught Enkidu? Do you think anyone misses him?"

Lazarus answers, "If he had anyone in his life, it was probably out of obligation, someone with a vested interest. He founded one the largest companies in the country but the media never spoke much about his personal life. I wonder what the news said when he disappeared. Someone like that doesn't just vanish without people taking notice."

The door beeps as we finish eating and the entrance opens. Having finished our meal, Zuri, Lazarus, and I stand up in anticipation. Twigs comes walking through the entryway. The hems of his light blue jumpsuit drag against the floor. He wears a hint of pride in his expression.

"Doug, you are next," Avi declares.

"See you in a bit." Lazarus gives me a pat on the back. Then he focuses his attention on Avi. "Coming," he says. He pads over to Avi and they both pass through the entryway. The guards follow behind, including those who had been overseeing our breakfast. Again, the doors close behind them, leaving Enkidu, Twigs, Zuri, and me free to roam.

AP-12 moves to our table and begins to clean up our dishes.

Zuri sighs and returns to her room, saying to me, "I'm still kind of tired. Maybe I can get some more sleep before it's my turn. Wake me up if anything exciting happens."

"Sure thing," I reply, watching as Zuri returns to our room.

Twigs seems to have calmed down, now beaming with confidence . He finds refuge in his room where he resumes his reading of The King in Yellow with a smile on his face.

I hear a whistle and direct my attention to the source of the sound. "What do you need, Enkidu?" I ask. His back is still against the wall and he beckons me over. I obey.

Drawing near to him, I see the excitement in his eyes. He grabs my wrist and pulls me closer. "This is very interesting. Things keep changing but not in an obvious way. Haven't you noticed the metamorphosis, the minuscule shift in the normalcy of our venue?" He begins to count on his fingers. "Avi, the final phase, strange humming: it is all a façade, a smokescreen to misdirect our attention. Surely a smart girl like you must have noticed by now?"

"I've noticed some of those things too," I admit. "I was really stiff when I woke up this morning, and that strange, vibrating hum — what do you think it is?"

"Oh, it is more than a hum," he tells me. "Here, feel this." He reaches for my hand and places it against the wall, putting his palm against the back of my hand and pushing with a gentle firmness. "Can you feel that?"

Before answering I close my eyes, letting my sense of touch take over. The wall quivers, soft and relaxing, sending delicate pulses through my fingertips, maintaining a soft steady rhythm, and communicating some foreign message. Eliciting Enkidu as my interpreter, I wonder, "What do you think it means? Do you think it is related to the humming sound?"

He explains. "It means we aren't stationary. We're moving! On a journey through an unknown space to an unknown place, we voyage. You know what I see: rolling waves of amber. It is our beginning, the reason for us being here. That is where we travel. The true question is not 'what.' We should be asking 'why' and 'where.'"

"You think we are moving?" I reflect on his words, paraphrasing them according to my understanding.

"Yes," he confirms.

"Well that doesn't make any sense. If we were moving, we'd feel more than a faint vibration. And not to mention that we're in a building, Enkidu," I insist. "It could be a generator or something like that. Maybe they need it to power some new equipment. They probably are just getting something ready for the final phase."

"Perhaps."

The door to the ward opens again, Lazarus returning. Avi comes a few seconds later, accompanied by his white-clad guards. He declares, "Gable, you are next".

"Coming, dear," Enkidu replies, chuckles, and marches out the door. Avi and the two guards follow him. Not more than a few seconds have passed when the door slides shut.

Without hesitation, Lazarus skulks into his room, seeming somewhat subdued. My heart beats faster and harder in my chest as I contemplate what this means. What are they asking us? What information does Avi hope to learn from his interactions?

I walk over to his room and enter. "Hey, are you alright?"

"I am," he confirms. "I'm just a little worn down. What Avi had me do in there was strange. I just wish I had all the answers about this place. Avi seems nice enough, but these new tests are physically draining."

"What kind of new tests?" I inquire.

He considers the question before responding. "Magic tests."

"Magic tests?" I raise an eyebrow. "What is that supposed to mean?"

"I'm not sure how to explain it. I wish I could understand things better myself. Then maybe I'd have more answers. Why would these scientists need to create people who can cast magic spells? The only reason I can logically accept is that they want us to fight someone. Or something." I can't tell if he's joking and am unsure how to respond, when he continues. "I'm pretty exhausted. Would it be okay if I rest up? We can talk more later. Then you can let me know how your test went."

"Sure." I leave the room, reflecting on what he's told me. Is there magic here? There have been some small changes, now that I think about things, how lately I've only had three hours of sleep each night and I've never felt tired or drained. Is that what the magic means?

Hoping to keep my mind occupied with happier thoughts, I see Zuri is still awake, sitting on her bed in our room. I skip over to it. Sticking my head into the room, I recognize she's writing in her journal and I ask, "I thought you were going to take a nap?"

"I was," she replies. "But thinking about guitars and music, I couldn't help but get creative. Look." She holds up her journal to reveal musical notes and lyrics to a song.

"Oh, that's cool!" I look at it. The piece is written in a 3/4 time signature, like most waltzes. I hum the melody: D4, D5, A4, A#4, D4, C5, G4, F4, G4, D4, D5, A4, A#4, C5, G4, A4, A#4, A4, F4, E4, F4, G4. "This is really good. You have a real talent for music. Have you considered doing this for a living? I mean before we were taken?"

"You really think it's good?"

"I do! It's really beautiful."

"Thanks," she says, hesitating before continuing. "These people who took us. I can't help but ask who they represent. Is it the government or some private organization? Do you think we will have more answers soon?" she asks.

"I don't know," I reply. "I hope so."

Zuri turns her attention back to her journal.

Deciding to leave her to her creativity, I step out of the room. As I leave, the main door sounds again – it is such an irritating sound, but at least it isn't a wailing siren or anything like that – and Enkidu is back. Unlike the others, he's wearing new clothes, a black business suit and dark red tie. Having seen him on national news more than once, it reminds me of the attire he wore during the early years of his company. Later on he began using lighter, earthier colors. But what is really puzzling to me is: why did they give him his clothes back? Is he the first one to go home?

"Amy, you are next." Avi looks at me and waits.

"On my way," I say, and follow him out the door, his guards taking their place behind me. As I pass by them, I confirm my suspicion — Avi's guards are indeed human.

We walk through the door which separates the ward from the rest of the facility and amble down the narrow hallway. It is made from the same material as the ward, no more than ten feet in any direction. Unlike the ward, however, the floor is a slate and marble checkered tile. The temperature seems cold compared to the ward.

We arrive outside the library. Pulling up the sleeve on his left arm, Avi reveals a metal band with countless squares and circles on a curved touch screen. They vary in size and color. As he taps them in sequence, the library door slides open and he addresses the guards, "Wait here". Shifting his attention back to me, he nods and steps into the library.

I take it to mean I'm supposed to follow him, so I do. He pushes a few more shapes on his wristband and the door slides shut behind him. A large rectangle, the library, stretches back forty or fifty feet:

sealed, white cubbies directly to our right. It is a spacious and luxurious white room. There is a small, circular table directly in front of us. Three padded chairs are placed around it. A beautiful glass chandelier hangs from the tall ceiling in the middle of the room. Aside from Avi and me, the library is eerily empty. "Where is everyone?" I ask.

"We've asked everyone to keep clear of the library today," Avi explains. "We'll be going over some of your personal information."

This room is a unique mix of past, present, and future. The past comes in the form of musty old hardbacks lining the walls and shelved in computerized compartments. The present comes in the form of traditional computers and flat screens which can display electronic copies of books. The future comes in as holograms and projections, 3D books which digitally re-enact the classic tales from world literature: Moby Dick, Journey to the West, Gilgamesh, Les Misérables, and The Count of Monte Cristo.

I walk over to a hologram representing Moby Dick and touch it. A light shoots from the point of my touch, creating a clear, life-size depiction of Captain Ahab directly in front of me. He stands at the helm of his ship as it bobs up and down in the water. The harpoon gun in his hands shifts back and forth, trying to find the white whale in the dark sea. I notice the floor beneath my feet shifts and fluctuates as if I was floating above the ocean.

Avi taps the hologram and the images fade to nothing. "Please, sit," he invites, pulling out one of the chairs from the table.

I plop down in the chair. It isn't a recliner but it is more comfortable than any furniture I have experienced in a very long time. Inhaling a deep breath, I let my body relax, relishing in the comfort.

Avi lifts his wrist, pushing on the band some more, and one of the cubbies slides out. He lifts it, carries it, and sets it atop the table. He places his hand on a biometrics scanner and the lid opens. Inside I see clothes: a full body suit, padded with some type of light-weight metal, like armor. It is made of a stretchy, form-fitting fabric. Gray bands run up the legs and arms of the otherwise white garment.

Avi explains, "I'll be back in five minutes. You may use the room near the back to change."

I nod.

Using his armband controls, he opens the door to the hall, and leaves, letting the door close behind him. I hear a few muffled voices in the hall and then a near perfect silence. The only sound is the strange, unidentifiable hum. It can't be an engine like Enkidu says.

I make my way to the back room and enter. In six months I'd rarely been left on my own. Having grown accustomed to being with others, it initially doesn't feel right to be somewhere by myself. Nonetheless, the awkwardness of privacy quickly passes and I remember how relaxing it is to be alone with my thoughts.

I change as quickly as I can. Once I'm in the new uniform it contracts to perfectly fit my body. It is more comfortable than I'd imagined it to be. I hear a knock at the door.

"Are you ready? It's time." Avi's voice communicates through an intercom. The door opens, I join him, and we exit into a hallway.

We continue further down into unfamiliar portions of the facility. As we round the corner, we reach a room with a sliding glass door. The door is open. Avi goes inside and I follow.

I am met by a large, dark, rectangular room. The panels in this room are the same size and shape but black. Dim green light spills from where the walls meet the ceiling. The wall directly in front of me has a row of glass panels. I can assume behind them that people watch the events in this room from the safety of their comfortable chairs.

Avi pulls something from his lab coat, holds it out, and asks, "What is this?"

"A glove," I retort.

He smiles – he wasn't supposed to smile – and explains. "The tests we've been doing should enhance your mind. Surely there is something else you can see here, aside from the basic details?"

Returning my gaze to the glove, I squint and look closer. The sooner I see what he wants, the sooner this will be over. It looks like a normal glove that matches my new uniform. I don't see anything unique. No logo, no unique design, regular accents; all of these things are common. What was different?

Closing my eyes and taking a few deep breaths to calm myself, I accidentally recognize the difference but not with my vision. I can feel something inside the glove, not cloth or thread. It is something else, and the item is no longer just a glove. My curiosity itches to know what is hidden within the lining of the cloth. It is familiar somehow; an energy, a presence.

"There is an energy to it."

"Exactly," he says, standing. "Put the glove on."

"Why?"

"It won't hurt you," he promises. "Put it on."

Knowing I have no choice, I slip the glove on and feel an instant boost. It reminds me of a caffeine high but it is more of an emotional sensation, not a physical one.

Avi then exits the room through a door disguised as one of the panels.

"Alright, Amy." I hear his voice over an intercom. "The test is about to begin. Are you ready?"

"Do I have a choice?" I answer. This is followed by a brief silence.

"Good luck," I hear him say.

A blue hologram appears, similar to the 3D image created by Moby Dick but without the detailed background. The image is that of a man without discernable details, just a glowing blue. He begins to run toward me.

Instinctively I raise my hand, feeling energy funnel through the glove, escaping from my fingertips. An arrow of light shoots forward. It finds its mark in the center of the hologram. In an explosion of light, the image dissipates and fades. This glove is a weapon. How am I controlling it?

Three more people take the place of the first and continue their predecessor's advance. One by one I blast each away, the third nearly upon me when its particles fade into nothing. Five new holograms appear and begin their charge.

Avi returns, taps his wristband, and the five illusions disappear. "That was all I needed to know today. I have one more thing before you return to the ward. AP-12 has it waiting for you in the ward."

He pushes his wrist band and a drawer slides from the wall next to the door. He reaches in, pulling out a blue jumpsuit, and tosses it to me. "You may change over there and then we will return to your room." He leaves, the door shutting behind him.

I change, leaving the white uniform and glove piled in the corner, and a few minutes later the door opens. Avi is standing outside. I follow him out to the hall and we begin to walk. We tread down the hall in silence. When we re-enter the ward I walk past him, and see his body stiffen. It is like he's as uneasy with me as I am with him.

After I pass him, he directs his attention to his guard. "That was our last test for the day." The guard nods and they turn to leave.

"Wait," I demand.

"Yes?"

"Aren't you going to take Zuri, now? She's the only one of us you haven't yet tested."

He ponders before replying. "I felt Prefect Gray would be more suited for her test."

"I see," I say, puzzled, as the door closes behind him. Doing a one-eighty, I search for Lazarus. He is standing in the doorway of his room, looking back at me. I nod and he smiles, waving me over.

Unsure of how to interpret his body language, I decide it is best to see what is going on. Hurrying over to him, I say, "What's up?"

"What did you think?" he inquires.

"What do you mean?"

"About the test," he says. "It felt strange. Why do you think they had us do that? Do you feel that we're being trained to fight too?"

I pause. "I'm not sure. It seems so, though."

"You don't seem tired," Lazarus observes.

"Should I be?"

He nods. "After I did Avi's test, I was worn out, like all my energy was drained. You don't seem affected. What did he have you do?"

I explained to him what Avi had me do. By his reaction, I take it his experience was different.

"What do you think the glove is? Some sort of plasma projectile weapon?" he asks.

"I don't think so," I state. "I think we are the weapon."

I make my way back to my room but am stopped prematurely as the light above the ward door blinks and the entryway opens, Prefect Gray stepping through. "Zuri," she says. "It is time for you to come with me." In the opening and closing of an eye my energy melts away, concern taking its place, upon hearing the tone in Prefect Gray's voice.

Enkidu comes over to me. He must be warming up, as he's never approached someone under his own free will before, not since I've known him. "You seem upset, Amy. That doesn't suit you. It makes your face wrinkle and your skin dry up... I don't know if what I just said is true but it might be. Now don't be a raisin and tell me...what's wrong?"

I explain. "Lazarus made me think about something. I don't get it... I had to do that glove test. When you did it, did you feel tired after or physically worn out?"

"I did," he confirms. "I'm still feeling drained."

"After I shot the holograms I didn't feel any different," I explain.

"You were able to shoot one?" Enkidu fixes his gaze on me. "Why would you do that? What did the poor holograms do to you?"

Ignoring his odd sense of humor, I say, "You know me, always proactive in eliminating my enemies". I wink.

"Not funny," he declares.

I insist. "I thought it was."

"You're wrong. It wasn't."

Chuckling, I ask, "But what do you think it all means? What makes me different from you and Lazarus? Should I worry? What is going on here?" Am I asking Enkidu for advice? What is wrong with me? I definitely don't feel myself. Enkidu chimes in.

"I can only guess what this all means, but I do have an idea. Did you ever read any of the recent studies done on human emotion?" he asks. I shake my head, so he continues, "They basically state that there are four primary human emotions: sadness, love, fear, and anger. My theory is that they are applying those concepts to us, instilling one of the primary emotions in each of us and using the other as a control. You are lucky, as it would so seem, that they picked you to be the one who is loved. Did they give you some present or a gift to remind you of some joyful moment?"

"Well, they said AP-12 had a present for me." I pause for a moment. "What emotion do you think you are?" I ask.

"It doesn't matter," he answers. I immediately recognize the somber tone in his voice and expression on his face. "The questions you should be asking, the questions I've been asking myself is – which is Lazarus? Which is Twigs? Which is Zuri? Zuri should be back from her visit with Prefect Gray any second. Maybe we'll have some more answers after she gets here."

Enkidu's words pierce me to the core, my heart sinks, and I try to grasp the context of what he's saying. If it is true, that they were testing emotions, it signifies that our situation might only be getting worse.

"Wait, how did you figure out they were doing these things?" I ask. "They just started the next phase of testing today."

Enkidu replies, "It is difficult to explain. Over the course of the last few weeks I have begun to have dreams of a sort. Images come to me and then those images become events in reality.

"Just be careful. I know I've told you it before but..." He hesitates, looking behind me. "Gotta go," he exclaims, a sudden panic in his voice. In the blink of an eye he is halfway up the steps, on the way to his room. The cause of his sudden escape reveals itself as Lazarus, who is only a few paces behind me. I guess Enkidu isn't ready to get close to anyone else yet.

"What's that dude's problem? Do you think Enkidu will ever warm up to me?" he questions.

I shake my head, with a smirk. "Probably not."

"Probably not," he agrees.

The door sounds again and cuts off our conversation, and the light above the entrance to the ward flashes as Zuri and two black guards return. They are carrying her and she's unconscious, wearing a white wedding dress. What significance does that have? What happened? I'm not sure. Nonetheless, the event is a resounding reminder. Whoever these scientists were, they were our enemy and we couldn't forget that.

CHAPTER TWO
BONDS

A few hours passed, nightfall approached, and Zuri hasn't come to. She isn't the same, a glazed fog in her eyes. She doesn't move from the spot the guards left her, which isn't the room we used to share.

The present AP-12 gave me was a guitar. I think Zuri will enjoy some company so I stay with her, playing the new instrument. Using her journal as a guide, I try out different variations of the song she wrote and mix things up with some of my favorites. She doesn't respond to anything. Giving up for the evening, I sigh, place the guitar against her wall, and return to my room.

The next morning I find Twigs sitting at the cafeteria table, finishing the last pages of the book he'd been reading. It is different than the one he's been keeping in his room. I wonder if the scientists know he's been reading The King in Yellow. They probably don't even realize he has it.

As I approach him he closes up the paperback and sets it on the table, a sinister grin spreading on his face. "Have you found the yellow sign?"

"Huh? What does that mean?" I ask.

"Nothing." The grin remains, a permanent unchanging feature on his face. I think he's finally lost it. "Enkidu finally told you they are playing with our emotions, didn't he?"

Taken aback, I answer, "Yes, he did. He told you too?"

"Enkidu just figured it out for himself, that they've been conditioning us. Do you know when I figured it out? I saw through all their games and tests six months ago, from day one. I know why you came to talk to me, Amy. You're trying to figure out the puzzle as well. You want to know which emotion they are using to test me. Which, if you found out, would give you a good clue as to what they are using to test Lazarus."

"I did," I confirm.

He folds his arms, lying them on the table. "Tonight, we will all know. Which of us is the control subject? Who are they driving to insanity through fear?" He laughs. "Soon we'll all know and you'll see how hopeless we really are."

I demand, "Twigs, tell me what you know! What have they done to you to make you so..." I consider my next word, careful to choose the right one, "...scared?"

He winks. "I'm not scared, as much as some people may hope for it."

Realizing I'm getting nowhere with him, I stand up and look for Lazarus.

From across the ward I see him in Zuri's new room, talking to her. As I approach, I realize that only Lazarus is talking.

I peek in and ask, "How is she doing?" Her eyes are still glazed and she hasn't left her bed since returning. I haven't even seen her sit up.

Lazarus doesn't respond.

I add, "Is there anything that I can do to help?" I hope for an answer but none comes. Zuri continues to lie on her bed, staring and lost, motionless. I wish I could help her. After all, I am her friend in this place. Sadness overcoming me, I back out of the room.

"Amy, wait," Lazarus insists.

He steps out to speak with me, saying, "Zuri just needs some extra support. She will come around. We just need to keep talking to her." His eyes gaze down at the floor. I've learned this look to mean he feels guilty for something and he confirms as much. "I wish I could do more to help her."

"This isn't anyone's fault and all we can do now is provide her moral support." We smile at each other.

He nods, and returns to Zuri's side, ending our conversation with, "I'll see you in the morning".

"I'll see you in the morning," I answer and turn around. Stepping past the table where Twigs sits, I decide to say goodnight to Enkidu, and begin moving toward the steps leading to the second level.

As I pass the table, Twigs chuckles, "Have you found the yellow sign?" Another giggle and he adds, "Classic".

Shrugging off his strange question, I make my way past AP-12, patting him on the head as I pass, and up the steps and to Enkidu. He lies in his bed, one eye open and one eye closed. "I know you're awake, Enkidu. I just wanted to say goodnight."

"I am awake," he admits.

I smile, hoping he will invite me in. There are so many things to talk about and so many questions in my head. He stares, a blank look on his face. It prompts me to leave. "Good night," I say to him and begin to walk away.

"I know you are still pursuing answers," he stops me. "Last night when you slept, your heart was whole. Tonight in your dreams it will be divided, confused and uncertain about what awaits. In your future it will have to learn to divide itself further and you will be responsible for more than just us in this prison. More than five people will depend on you. Learn to stick to your convictions. Never stray from the path that is yours, one of caring for others. It is what makes you who you are, your greatest asset."

"Does anything you say ever make sense?" I ask, turning to face him,

"It always makes sense but usually in retrospect, only after the future has turned to past and what I've said has become a fulfilled prophecy. It is like I told you earlier. I see things in my dreams sometimes. If you want increased insight into things to come, you have to listen with your feelings and with your heart. The problem is — it whispers, so you have to listen closely."

I ponder his advice, considering all the things which have happened today and ask, "You're sadness, aren't you?"

He refuses to answer and feigns that he doesn't understand the question, completely avoiding eye contact.

"Enkidu, you can talk to me. I saw how you reacted when I asked earlier. What have they done to you?" He squeezes his eyes together, as if deciding how to answer. "Come on. You can trust me."

He pauses for a moment. Reaching into the pocket of his new, light brown suit, he pulls out a picture of a little girl and holds it out to me. I take it, inspecting the image. "Her name was Phoenix," he says. "She was my daughter."

Sympathetic to the fact he's speaking in the past tense, I comment, "She was very beautiful".

Tears forming in his eyes, he takes the image back and returns it to his pocket. "I used to wear lighter suits, browns and grays. After she was gone, I felt empty. I no longer felt safe in the world. It is a cruel, horrible place. From that day on I only wore black, to represent how I feel on the inside.

"Now, enough about me and my past. No doubt, you've seen what they did to Zuri. I wonder how the dress plays a part in this?"

It would be nice to know what emotion Zuri was given, as it would help us better understand which emotions remained for Twigs and Lazarus. Thinking about Twigs, I say, "Twigs seems to have fallen off the deep end. He kept asking me if I had found the yellow sign and smiling about it. It was really creepy. Something is very wrong with that kid."

Enkidu says, "He's a sociopath...a very smart one. Now he seems to be delusional too. The question he asked isn't a sign of fear in him. The yellow sign is well known in some cultures. It is a symbol and a curse, indicating that something bad is about to happen.

"You've noticed the book he's been reading in his room?" he asks.

I nod.

"I think he may be fear because of that book," he suggests.

"No," I submit. "The book he's been reading doesn't have the library markings. It is something he obtained on his own. I doubt the science teams even know he has it."

He scratches his head.

I look down at Zuri's new room. "It looks like Lazarus is still there. Hopefully, he can help her."

"Nah, no one can help her, not anymore. She's beyond that. Poor girl."

I sigh. "Anyway, the lights will go out soon. I'm headed to bed. Have a good night."

"No such thing as a good night for me, not anymore. I don't get any good days either. Glad someone still does." He forces a smile.

"Good night," I repeat, squeezing his shoulder. The instant I touch his shoulder, I feel his emotions flow into me. The sorrow is overwhelming. I release my grip and turn to leave, casting my eyes back on Enkidu one more time. He's lying back on his bed, both eyes closed. Did I really just feel his emotions? That's impossible, but it felt so real. So sad.

Before long I am back in my room, the lights are out, and I am drifting off to sleep. I am with my family. My brother Tom and I are playing cards together and eating sugar cubes outside in the park. The rest of my family is around us, playing catch with a football. The warm sun kisses my skin, a calm breeze against my face. It feels so good to be outside again.

I notice a caterpillar crawling across our picnic table. "How do you do today?" it asks. "Have you come to join our tea party? The others should be here shortly."

Without any odd reaction to a caterpillar talking to me, I exclaim, "I would love to! I have some crumpets!" and they magically appear on the table.

"Oh, those look lovely," he says, asking, "Have you seen my friends? Have you found the yellow sign?"

Adrenaline shoots through me, causing my heart to race. I hear a strange gurgle and glance up at my brother. His face has decayed, empty sockets in place of eyes. The hollowness of them is turned upward, examining the sky. His mouth is open wide, the jaw dislocated on one side.

Turning my eyes away from Tom, I see my little brother. He has undergone the same transformation, decaying and rotting away in front of my eyes, standing two meters away. I hear his voice. "Amy, why did you leave us?"

Returning my attention to Tom, as if in one sudden movement, he is directly in front of me, his mouth open unnaturally wide. He screams. I bolt upright in my bed, breathing heavily and covered in a cold sweat.

I realize the shrill scream piercing through the night is not just part of a dream but also a reality. Adrenaline continues to sharpen my senses as I realize I was dreaming. But it doesn't take long to understand that the screams are real. I instantly realize the sound is coming from my brother Lazarus.

Jumping out of my bed and running to his room, I am the first one there. His room is completely empty. His bed is missing but his screams emanate from beneath the tiles where it once stood. He is buried beneath the floor. I notice his bed, which had been attached to the wall, is no longer there. It must have fallen down into the floor as he slept.

Now there are no latches or handles. I pound against the floor, anxiety building in my chest. My heart beats stronger and I continue to find a way to free him.

"Lazarus, can you hear me?" I try to reach him but to no avail.

"Please, it is going to be okay. I'm here. Talk to me!"

Over the shouting, I doubt my words can be heard. Remembering my test with Avi and the glove, a hope spawns within me. Maybe I can use magic to release Lazarus.

Observing the angles and surface of the trap, every visual detail, I prepare. Then I close my eyes and sense everything on a different level, connecting with Lazarus. Terror floods into me: a fear of the dark and a fear of worms. I am covered in them. What am I feeling? I've never been afraid of those things before. Now the thought of them is petrifying.

I feel it is hopeless, that there is no way to get him out. The only support I can provide him is of the moral variety. With each second I hope he will calm. With each minute I hope the floor will release him, but he continues to yell, his shrieks carrying through the night.

Then I understand – the dark and the worms – those are his fears and not mine. Forcing calm into myself and pushing it into him, I feel him relax. "Lazarus," I project my thoughts, "It's your sister Amy. Can you hear me?"

"HELP ME!" He returns the message. "What is going on? Where am I? HELP ME!"

"You are still in the ward with us. Somehow they trapped you beneath the floor. There are no handles or anything, no physical way to open it. I have an idea, though."

"What?" he asks. "PLEASE HELP ME!"

"It's okay." I try to calm him. "I think we can free you if we focus our minds and do it together."

"I'll try," he answers.

Breaking communication, I put all my attention on the floor. I imagine it opening and nothing happens. Refusing to give up, I make another concerted effort.

It remains unmoving.

Returning to a focus on the physical, I see AP-12 next to me, running his hand over the wall next to where the bed had been. The floor begins to open.

I peer into the opening. Once fully open, the bed begins to rise. Lazarus is panting, worn down from the exertion of magic. I don't even feel winded. I reach in to help him out and realize that he's not covered in worms, not physically. They are in his mind somehow.

Lazarus's hand meets mine and he uses it as leverage and we pull. Our combined efforts are not enough to lift him. "Hang in there, Lazarus," I tell him. "We are so close."

Lazarus pulls himself up onto the floor and I sit next to him. He has tears in his eyes and I can feel some forming in my own. I place my hand on his cheek, saying, "I'm glad you're okay," and I pull him in close.

He wraps his arms around me, burying his face in my shoulder. I return the act in kind and there we remain, embracing in the darkness.

AP-12 apologizes. "I'm sorry. I hadn't realized they planned to do that. Had I known, I wouldn't have allowed it. It won't happen again. Good night."

We hold each other in the corner of his room until the next morning. Raising my head off his shoulder, I ask Lazarus, "Are you okay?"

"I am alright, rattled, but alright. I never told anyone I was afraid of the dark before, nor that I hate worms," Lazarus answers. "I don't know how they found out. I think I just need some time to myself now."

Looking into his eyes, I decide to obey his command, giving him a moment to recover on his own. I kiss his forehead good bye and leave him, finding my way to the dining table.

Time goes by, but lost in thought, it is hard to tell how much. Eventually, Lazarus leaves his room and I join him at the table. Little by little we begin to converse but not about last night. He seems to prefer avoiding the topic. I can't blame him.

Zuri doesn't join us, and still hasn't left her bed. AP-12 delivers our food, and Lazarus stirs his mush of oats, never lifting his spoon to his mouth. Far from us, Enkidu eats in his usual spot. His eyes meet mine and I mouth, "Thank you". He smiles.

A loudspeaker cuts into our breakfast, Avi's voice coming over it.

"Today we will be doing follow-up evaluations. Amy, you will be first. Today's tests will be significantly longer than yesterday."

I give Lazarus a hug before standing and shouting back at the loudspeaker, angered by last night's events. "I really don't feel like talking today. But since I know you aren't going to give me a choice, we may as well get it over with."

"Yes, we may as well," Avi repeats, still over the loudspeaker. He was either ignoring the sarcasm in my tone or he simply didn't understand it. "The guards will bring you to your next test. They are waiting outside the door," he says. The door beeps and opens.

I find Avi's white-clad guards outside the door. The trip to the library is made in silence. Using an armband, the guard opens the library, and steps aside. "After you," he insists.

Slipping past him, I take a seat in the same chair where I sat yesterday and scowl, my heart set on making the testing process as difficult as possible. "No, not there," the guard explains, pointing to an open door in the back of the library. I don't remember that door being there before.

I walk through the doorway and find myself in a small bright room with a simple chair. "Thank you for coming," Avi's voice says over a speaker, the door sealing shut and leaving me trapped in the tiny space. I sit in the chair. Directly in front of me is a dark, mirrored glass reflecting my image back at me. It's been so long since I've seen myself. My face seems different in so many ways: a cautious expression, clarity in my eyes, full lips, a perfect complexion without wrinkles or blemish. Is that really me? I stand, moving toward the glass until I'm a few inches away. I've always been critical of my appearance but now I find no flaws. Staring into my eyes, I feel my cheeks with the palms of my hands. They feel so soft. It is strangely comforting and at the same time off-putting. What have they done to me?

"Are you okay?" Avi's voice breaks my train of thought, bringing me back to reality like cold water being poured down my back.

I blink, returning to my senses.

"Amy?" he asks.

Anger replaces awe and I explode. "Twigs was right about you!"

"What do you mean?"

"You only care about yourself!" I glare through the glass at him and pound it. As if responding to my anger, the chair flies back and against the wall. "What you did to Lazarus is unthinkable. He wouldn't do anything to hurt a fly. I'm not stupid, none of us are. Don't insult our intelligence and don't even think about doing that to my brother again!"

Overwhelming sadness replaces anger and I collapse to the floor, covering my face with my hands and weeping. The door to the interrogation area opens and I hear someone's footsteps pass through the doorway. I keep my head in my palms. Kneeling next to me, the person puts his arm around my shoulder – an act of comfort.

Looking up, I see Avi. For the first time since I've met him, I see Avi as a human. His face is blushing. He seems ashamed.

Sensing this change in Avi, I begin to wonder. Did he care what we thought about him? His reaction indicates as much. It confuses me. How can he care about us and what I think, and then have such disregard for our wellbeing? What are they really doing to us? Remembering yesterday, I realize he has more of a heart than I am giving him credit for. After all, he couldn't bring himself to be the one to examine Zuri. He may have even thought that Enkidu would appreciate a picture of his daughter. Still, what they did to Lazarus is unforgivable.

The door to the interrogation room slides open once again and Prefect Gray enters. "That is quite enough. I want to see you in my office, Dr. Taylor. Now. Guards, return Amy to the ward."

Sitting at the table where we eat, I share the incident with Lazarus.

"Amy," he whispers. I look at him. "Don't be so quick to judge Avi. I can't explain it, but you have to trust me on this. Avi is on our side. I know he is. What happened to me last night isn't his fault."

"What do you mean?" I ask.

"If you trust me then trust him." He hesitates, looking around, and then adds, "I really can't say anymore. There are ears everywhere."

AP-12 whizzes by, whistling a tune.

"Okay. I trust you," I stammer, his advice catching me off guard. Refocusing on the exit, I inch forward and consider what Lazarus just told me. How can he be so quick to forgive Avi after last night? Still, if there is any one person I can trust, it is Lazarus. He must know something that I don't.

"Good." He stands. "I'm going to check on Zuri."

"How is she?" I ask.

"Still the same. She hasn't said anything and hasn't moved. I am concerned that she may need medical attention soon if she doesn't start responding." He walks away.

I am alone at the table. That is, until Twigs draws near and prods, "Why did they only have a follow-up test with you? He didn't want to talk to the rest of us? No, that's not it. He has feelings for you and you have tainted his judgment, compromised the entire six-month experiment we have been a part of. I bet Prefect Gray doesn't like that."

"Please, leave me alone. That's ridiculous," I snap.

He continues, "There is no fun in that". He looks up at me. "Did you know Lazarus is still trying to help Zuri, talking to her in her room? She's beyond help, though. Lazarus won't be able to help her."

"Twigs, if I wanted to hear ranting, I'd be with Enkidu." I glance up at Enkidu's room. "I have a lot to think about right now. Just please, leave me alone."

"Oh, Amy. You don't have all the pieces to complete your mental puzzle. But guess what? I do. You know how Lazarus always tells you there are things that are better not to know? Regarding Ais and Apollyon? I know what they are and I understand what they mean for our future and our freedom. Has your magic grown, yet? It has in the others."

I ignore his questions. "Stop taunting me, Twigs."

"I will tell you," Twigs snickers. "Only because it will give you more questions and deepen your nightmares. Even for someone as smart as I am, they both are hard to imagine being real."

I stare at him without saying a word. In one sense, I want to stand up and leave. In another sense, my curiosity has got hold of me. Does he really know what Lazarus keeps talking about in his sleep?

Twigs smiles. "They are simple concepts, really, Ais and Apollyon. To understand them you have to understand who we are and what we are being made into. The food they feed us is how they've improved our bodies, polluting our blood with pico-technology. Tiny, tiny robots, smaller than red blood cells. It reacts with our biology, giving us the ability to access every ounce of our minds and control every sinew in our body."

"Stop being so cryptic," I demand.

He explains, "I'm not being cryptic. They are using this technology to increase our brain power and give us special abilities that no other human being can have. By doing so, these scientists are literally creating 'magic' in us. Don't tell me you haven't felt different: heightened senses, more stamina, and increased reasoning. I mean, you felt it with Lazarus last night, didn't you? While you were trying to rescue him?"

Unable to formulate a response, I am attempting to process what he's saying. From one day to the next I haven't noticed any of the changes he mentioned...but seeing the bigger picture...I have definitely become more athletic and had an increased clarity of thought when compared to my abilities six months ago. Twigs must have noticed the process of thought and reasoning in my expression. He looks at me and smiles, "Yes, magic is real. So are Ais and Apollyon."

Twigs laughs. "Amy, the big sister I never had," he taunts. "The problem the scientists have come across is the deterioration of the human mind. A mortal body was never designed to harbor this unnatural gift." He grins: sinister, apathetic, and without remorse.

"The others who were with us before were too weak, mentally and physically, to contain this 'magic' within themselves. As the technology fused with their brains, they began to break down, and they were taken, one by one. What is interesting is why the five of us have survived this long. And what did they do with the others? What a waste to let their deaths be in vain, though. Wouldn't you agree? Prefect Gray and her lackeys certainly felt that way, and so they started the development of a new process, one which takes the soul of a person, now digitized by the pico-technology, and places it into an object: a ring, necklace, book, gemstone, any piece of jewelry, so on and so forth."

I stop him. "Wait, are you saying that they have figured out a way to transfer a person's soul into an inanimate object? That can't be possible." Is that where everyone went? Are their bodies dead and their spirits trapped?

Twigs giggles. "It is possible and they've done it more times than you can count. They are called Ais, the reciprocals containing the spirits of the dead...or maybe I should say the spirits of the ever living. I suppose it doesn't matter. Lazarus knows about the Ais because he has been converted into one and then shifted back into his body before it physically dies. He said he could see and hear while he was an Ai, explained that he watched his motionless, soulless body. Shifting back and forth, he spent time in the afterlife, or a form of afterlife. He described it as purgatory, a place where one cannot progress or move forward. It is called Apollyon."

My mind feels numb. None of what he says makes sense and so I argue. "That can't be true. People who have had near death experiences have never mentioned such a place before."

"Haven't you been paying attention? Apollyon is our special hell. We are no longer one hundred percent biological! This new afterlife is for magic users and Ais. Lazarus and I believe that this place created it." Twigs pauses. "As far as Apollyon goes, the only sure thing we know about it is that it exists. Beyond that we are left to speculation about its creation and purpose."

I don't know what to make of what Twigs just said. I sigh and stand, planning to return to my room. It will be good to gather my thoughts by myself. Twigs was not going to help ease my mind.

Before I reach my room, a tremor shakes the facility, knocking me off my feet. I retreat back to the table, crouching beneath it alongside of Twigs. Adrenaline turns to despair as I wait and hope for the quaking to stop.

The shaking seems to go on forever. When the trembling finally stops, it leaves us in an unusual silence, my mind guessing as to the cause of the vibrations. Twigs finally breaks the quiet, saying with a cheerful intonation, "Now, things are about to get very interesting".

CHAPTER THREE
DISCOVERIES

That night AP-12 makes us pizza for dinner, the first time we've had normal food in months. We eat and then go to bed, Lazarus spending the twilight hours with Zuri once more. I'm worried for them both. We still haven't talked about what happened to him the other night. Maybe he'd prefer not talk about it.

My overactive mind impedes sleep as I ponder the events of the last two days. It is disturbing and devastating to realize how quickly things have changed. Hopefully, Lazarus will open up to me tomorrow. If he doesn't want to talk about how he'd been tormented, I won't push. I want to know if what Twigs told me was true, about Ais and Apollyon. Did they transpose the spirits of our friends into simple pieces of jewelry and objects? The thoughts pollute my subconscious and when I find sleep, my dreams are filled with every insecurity and fear.

I awake to the soft whisper of my name, "Amy...Amy...wake up, Amy!" Opening my eyes, I see Avi over me and almost scream. As if anticipating this, he holds his finger to his lips, saying, "Shh...I have something to show you. I wanted to answer your questions before but Prefect Gray wouldn't allow it. If you come with me now, tonight, I can show you everything and no one will ever have to know."

"You're crazy," I whisper. "How do I know you aren't tricking me? Sorry, I feel much safer right here."

"It has nothing to do with trickery. Who do you think programmed AP-12 to save Lazarus earlier?" He lets the question sink in before adding, "The security system and cameras are rebooting after the earthquake earlier. Who knows how much longer they will be down. So are you coming?"

"I am." The words leave my mouth, remembering Lazarus's advice and adding it to Avi's assertion that he programmed AP-12 to help my brother.

"Good." He maneuvers his way out the room, careful not to make a sound.

I stand up and follow: keeping quiet, shunting away the fear of what may happen, and hoping for enlightenment.

We leave the ward and tiptoe down the hall. We pass the library. Just as the temperature decreased from ward to hallway, from the library on it continues to drop. Before long we turn around a 90 degree angle and are on light gray carpet. Passing so many doors that I lose count, I ask, "Where do these go?"

"Living quarters for the scientists," he whispers. "We're almost to mine. It is better if we talk there, less likely we'll get caught." Tension remains high as we reach a door at the end of the hall. "Here we are." He taps his armband, unlocking the door, and pushes it open. "Please, come in."

"After you," I insist.

"As you wish." He goes into the room and I follow, closing the door behind me. Softly, it clicks shut. As the light is turned on, my senses are comforted in the familiar set-up of a home environment: chairs, a piano, pictures on the walls, a thermostat, a love seat, and a sofa. What makes Avi's living space unique is the overabundance of puzzles, building blocks, and blueprints. Strange machines sit on a table in the back left corner. The air smells like incense. The same gray carpet extends in from the hallway. Knowing that the scientists live so well compared to us, it is hard not to feel offended.

Avi opens a closet door. He takes off his coat and hangs it up. Under the coat he wears a tight black t-shirt and black jeans. Seeing him in casual clothes, he seems more normal. He walks to a cabinet and opens it, reaches in, and pulls something out.

"We don't have much time, so please have a seat. This, Amy, is an Ai. I know you are aware of what they are. AP-12 informed me Twigs told you," he explains, handing it to me. I hesitate and he encourages, "Take it. You'll understand better if you see what it is for yourself."

I take it from him and let it sit in my palm, examining it. It is a thin gold chain, nothing to set it apart from any other necklace, no engravings or inlaid gems. Still, something about the object feels special — important. A few seconds pass and the sentiment of importance gains a physical manifestation, the necklace beginning to glow. The aura is a warm yellow and familiar.

Avi says, "The human mind is inherently subject to the corruption of power and what we have been giving you and your friends is ultimate power. When a person taps into that power, it can break their mind, corrupt it. Your friend, Olivia, unfortunately was at that point. Do you remember how she was?"

Entranced with the light, I answer. "I do. She was so sad and wanted to go home. Every minute of every day she begged the guards to let her go. Her sadness turned to anger and then suddenly — she no longer begged. That is when they came and got her, telling her they were going to help her, and taking her from the ward. I never saw her again."

"Right," Avi starts. "If they didn't do something to save her mind she would have been completely lost, her humanity gone forever. They took her spirit and mind, transferring it to this necklace. She goes by 'Artemis' now. Go ahead and talk to her."

What he is telling me echoes what Twigs said about Ais. It is terrifying and mystical all at once, giving way to so many new questions. Would there be a way to return her to her body, or had her body died? If this is all true, when Lazarus's spirit had left his physical self over and over again, was he being put in something else while his body lay motionless? Figuring it is best to hold all questions until Avi has finished explaining, I hold the necklace up to my face and say, "Artemis?"

The necklace's luminosity fluctuates as if responding to my voice but nothing else happens. Avi tells me, "Keep speaking. She can hear you and see you. Ais can be shy, though. They aren't quite sure why, yet. It is part of what they are trying to figure out here."

"Artemis, are you there? It's me, Amy." Silence prevails and I wait: patient, curious, and anxious all at once. When no response comes, I add, "We used to be friends. Don't you remember me?" Still nothing. Disheartened, I petition, "Please, talk to me. Do something to let me know you're there."

I am about to give up when I hear a soft ethereal voice, shy at first. "Amy, I am here. I can hear you, and I remember our friendship. How are you here? They've kept us away from you. They don't want anyone to know about us, not unless they are about to join us. Are you alright?"

Tears begin to form in my eyes upon being united with my old friend.

"Don't be sad, Amy. What happened to me and the others won't happen to you. You're different. I always knew it. You need to tap into the magic inside of you and figure out how to use it to get out of this place."

"Is Artemis speaking to you?" Avi interrupts. "Can you hear her?"

"She is." I confirm, puzzled why he is asking me such an obvious question.

"Good," Avi says, smiling. "Ais can only communicate through physical contact with someone who harbors the pico-technology. I have to wear a special glove, which I've created, in order to hear what is being said."

He gestures to a glove fitted on a model hand nearby.

"Prefect Gray knows the power they contain but is unaware that they are able to communicate. That's our little secret. I want you to keep Artemis with you. Be careful not to let anyone else know you have her. It is obvious you two are good for one another."

"What do you mean?" I ask.

"You are good for her because you've helped her to open up. She's never spoken to me before. Some of the other Ais are much more willing to talk to me but she never was." His face is brightened by Artemis's glow.

"I can tell Artemis is good for you because you are glowing, literally. Look." I look down at my arms, and sure enough my body has begun to glow the same type of glow as the necklace. Every inch of me radiates the glow, and the extent of the light's reach grows with my delight at seeing it. The light seems to be emanating from beneath my skin, as if there is iridescent liquid in my veins.

Aside from the apparent change in appearance, I do feel myself connecting to something deeper inside of me, an energy source and power. It rejuvenates me in an instant and I can't help but know things are going to be okay.

Avi smiles, "Beautiful".

I feel myself blushing and wonder how the red in my cheeks combines with the yellow aura around me.

As if realizing what he's said, he rescinds and refocuses on the topic at hand. "Tomorrow they have scheduled to take your brother and subject him to the final test. I am working on a plan to get us all out of this terrible place. If all goes well, Lazarus will be unharmed, and we can make our escape."

I feel like so many of my questions were answered tonight but twice the amount have taken their place. Avi must see me struggling to understand everything.

"No time to explain now," Avi states before I can say a word. "I will come find you tomorrow when it's time. AP-12 will give you further instructions. We have to go now. Keep Artemis safe. I will do my best to make sure we all get out of this alive."

I put the necklace in my pocket. My eyes meet his and their sincerity shines back at me. He smiles. "Let's get back to your room. I don't know how much longer until security protocols re-initiate and the last thing either of us needs is for Prefect Gray to know about our meeting tonight."

We make our way back to my room, careful not to disturb anyone. Arriving at my room, I smile at Avi. Do I thank him? I am not sure what to feel. As he pulls away to leave he whispers a final piece of advice, "Amy, be careful. Tomorrow everything changes."

I am not able to sleep, again tonight and so I begin my morning walk earlier than usual. Zuri remains in the same bed where the guards placed her, catatonic and broken. She even looks a little paler. My heart goes out to her and I wish I could help. Lazarus trusted

AP-12 to not let the incident from two nights before repeat and is asleep in his room. Twigs sleeps in his, curled up and completely blanketed. Stepping up the stairway, I find Enkidu sitting on his bed. Before I can say anything he speaks, echoing Avi's prophecy. "Today is the day when everything changes."

"You heard Avi say that?" I ask.

Enkidu blinks, confused. "No, I didn't hear him say anything but I did see you with him last night, sneaking away into the darkness. What was that about?" I feel the blood rush to my head. "Now you're blushing. Did something happen last night that I need to know about?"

"Something happened," I confess, "but nothing like what you think. I learned a lot about this place. Avi shared some dark secrets. If you didn't hear what Avi was telling me, why do you think today is the day when everything changes?"

"Come here and I'll show you." He waves me over. I move close and he takes my hand in a gentle grip, pushing it against the wall and holding it there. The vibration I felt the other day is gone.

"We're here," he explains.

After what I had seen with Artemis, I would believe just about anything. Still, moving buildings is something I'm not ready to accept, no matter how strong a case Enkidu makes for them.

The lights turn on and a loudspeaker blares out Prefect Gray's voice. It sounds oddly cheery.

"Good morning. After breakfast we will be concluding the evaluations from yesterday. We hope to have the final phase underway sometime later today. Isn't that wonderful? Please, enjoy our very special breakfast which we have prepared for you today. AP-12 will be along to deliver it shortly." Her voice squeaks with excitement.

"We are on the cusp of all we have been working toward. We thank you for all that you have done. My heartfelt thanks." She pauses for dramatic effect, adding, "Hoorah!" The speakers click off, but her final word resonated in the acoustics of the ward.

"I don't like her at all," Enkidu comments. "Gray is not the right color for her. If it were up to me I would have named her Prefect Black. It is a color which suits her better, dark like she is...the evil witch. She relishes in a success which she may never see."

Intrigued by his odd perceptiveness and the accuracy of his past prophecies, I decide to pry. "Oh, really? What makes you think she may never see it? Where do these divinations come from?"

He smirks. "Like I said before, they come as images. They are becoming clearer as of last night. Some I am beginning to see just as clearly as I'm seeing you. If only the visions would have come sooner in life. I could have made a fortune betting on sports."

"You were already a billionaire," I quip. "It isn't like you needed the money."

He chuckles and admits, "Sharp as a tack, you are. Life is a lot more than money, my dear."

The door buzzes and AP-12 comes in with two robot guards, bringing our food. He places the boxes on our table. Then he hands me a trinket, whispering, "It is a ninja turtle, like your brother". It puts a smile on my face. He then he moves to empty rooms, beginning his daily cleaning routine. The robot guards stand alert, one on each side of the door.

"Race you downstairs," Enkidu challenges me, and we hurry down to the meal table.

I beat Enkidu to the table. Pancakes! Anxious to discover what toppings our special pancake breakfast may include, I pull off the lid on one of the containers. Unfortunately, they only come with butter.

Even so, the prospect of soft warm pancakes with melted butter is enough to lift my spirits.

Leaving his room, Lazarus comes over, and sits next to me, muttering, "Good morning".

"Good morning," I say, glancing across at him. He looks better today, like the fog in his eyes is leaving. Getting a full night's sleep did him good…and not being tortured at night…that probably helped, too. "So today is the big day. At least that is what everyone says. Do you have any idea what the final phase is?"

Thinking for a few seconds, he finally replies. "I don't have any clear-cut idea what it is."

"Are you nervous?" I whisper. My anxiety increases, not knowing what they want to do to my brother, but hopeful that this escape plan will work. Maybe we won't have to find out.

"No, it doesn't make me nervous," he insists. His wavering tone suggests otherwise.

Not sure how to follow up, I begin to eat my pancake. Glancing up, I notice the ceiling windows are open, allowing natural light to shine through once again. The sky seems unusually bright, bluer than usual…a cloudless cerulean. Enkidu creeps by, snatching up some pancakes and walking to his usual spot against the wall where he will eat. I ask Lazarus, "How's Zuri?"

"She's not Zuri anymore," he says.

I rub his back and glance back up at the windows. Just then, my heart skips a beat when I see that a face is there, staring back. It isn't human, nor does it belong to any animal I recognize. Whatever the creature is, its face fills the window for a few more seconds and then it is gone.

The sudden jump in my arm tips Lazarus off to the fact that something isn't right. "What is it?" he asks, following my gaze until he's looking at the window.

"I just saw something...I don't know what it was."

Lazarus reassures me. "I bet it was nothing. Is Twigs going to join us to eat?"

Bringing my attention back to Lazarus I say, "I'll go ask him".

Before I can stand, the ward's door beeps. Prefect Gray steps through with no sign of Avi. "Doug," Prefect Gray says, "it is time to go."

Kissing my forehead goodbye, Lazarus stands and says, "Don't worry. Things will be okay." I see him give me one final glance, a wink, and watch as he walks out the door. My heart aches.

Hours pass and Twigs still hasn't left his room. With Zuri unmoving and Lazarus with the scientists, it leaves me to speak with Enkidu...or with the two guards who were assigned to guard the ward's door. It wasn't a normal practice to have them stay with us and I can't help but wonder if their presence has something to do with Avi and me the night before. AP-12 never talked when other robots were in the room, like they made him nervous or something.

At this point in time I don't know what to say to Enkidu. Worrying about Lazarus, it is difficult for me to remain calm and think logically. A strange eeriness emanates from the guards, like they are programmed to be on high alert after what happened...or because of what is about to happen. Is it possible for robots to be scared? Pacing back and forth and reaching my hand into my pants pocket, I find my new necklace and roll the chain back and forth between my fingers, a nervous habit.

Enkidu advises, "Don't worry, Amy. We both knew that today would be the day when everything changed. You need to keep a clear head if we're going to make it out of this alive." He shifts his eyes down. "What's that in your pocket?"

I remember Avi's advice not to tell anyone about Artemis. Pulling it out of my pocket, I show it to him and say, "Oh, this? It's just a necklace. I used to have one like it before. AP-12 made it for me the other day."

"I've seen the crap he makes. That's not his. Did your other necklace glow?" Enkidu asks, squinting his eyes to get a better look. "Because this necklace just started to glow. Don't lie to me, Amy. You're the only person I still like, remember? We don't need to go messing that up. Now, tell me what that is. Is it an Ai?"

Feeling guilty for being caught, my shoulders slump, I relent, and admit, "I'm sorry, Enkidu. Yes, it is an Ai. It's Olivia. Now, she goes by 'Artemis. She can hear you and see you. If she decides to she can even talk to you."

Leaning in closer, he says, "This is incredible. Avi gave this to you last night? So he is looking out for our best interests? That is good to know."

"Enkidu..." I pause, and take a deep breath. "How is it that Lazarus, Twigs, and you all knew about the Ais before? Knowing what they are and what happened to our friends, how were you able to keep going? Knowing that this could be your fate?"

"Amy, we are different than you. You think with your heart and carry the weight of the world on your shoulders. None of us told you because we knew it would pull at your heart strings. How we found out doesn't matter. What does matter is what you will do now that you've discovered the truth. Will you despair or will you use it as fuel, a means to power onward?"

Without hesitating, I answer. "I guess I don't have much of a choice. Why haven't you, Twigs, Zuri, Lazarus, and I been turned into Ais yet? Why haven't we broken down like the others? Is it because we are mentally stronger than the others?"

Enkidu shrugs in confusion.

I continue. "At least, that is how Avi made it sound. Enkidu, whatever the final phase is, we stick together and get past it...right?"

"I wish it were that simple but some of us are already lost. Nonetheless, you and I: we are in this together. I'm on your side and I will not leave you alone." Enkidu puts his hand on my shoulder.

I soften my voice and lean closer. "You know that Avi is trying to get us all out of here today? He told me last night."

"Nonsense. There is no way he could get us out of here. And where exactly is 'here' anyways? Lazarus was brave." Enkidu can't keep eye contact. "When he left with those scientists...he knew he wasn't coming back."

My heart drops. "You're wrong. He will be back, and Avi will rescue us," I insist.

Enkidu smiles. "Maybe he will be. Maybe we will be rescued. But I'm usually always right, though. I'm sorry, Amy."

Artemis finally joins the conversation. "Hold me out to Enkidu so that he can hear me."

"Enkidu, hold my hand," I ask.

"What?" He wrinkles his forehead. "Ah, I think you're getting the wrong idea about our relationship."

I roll my eyes, demanding, "Hold my hand". I reach out, interlocking my fingers in his.

Now in contact with Enkidu, Artemis says, "Well, hello, Enkidu. You say you hope you are wrong. But your words don't sound very sincere. As an Ai, I wasn't privy to details about the final phase. But I was closer to it than you. In my opinion, it had something to do with using Lazarus's magic to protect the facility. As Ais we can amplify magical energy but can't produce it by ourselves. In other words, they will need to keep Lazarus alive if they want him to be using any magic. I think he'll be back."

"Look at that," Enkidu says. "The Ai can talk. I don't mean to sound rude but how do you know this is Olivia? It could be something else. It might be a bad influence on you." He raises an eyebrow.

"I'm not a bad influence," Artemis declares.

"Bad influence!" Enkidu quips.

Artemis responds, "Better to be a bad influence than a grumpy old man. Before I became an Ai, you never talked to anyone. It looks like you've finally opened up to Amy, which isn't much of an accomplishment. She's kind of the nicest person ever. So did you ever extend your circle of friends to include anyone else? You don't care if Lazarus comes back because you don't care about Lazarus. Amy, on the other hand, doesn't give up on people as easily as you!"

"Bad influence!"

I intercede. "Guys, arguing won't help anyone. If you keep this up they will overhear you." I nod toward the guards. "If they figured out we know more about the experiments than we're supposed to, it won't be a good thing."

"I didn't start it," Enkidu and Artemis say in unison.

Their argument is cut short by a rumble in the distance. It is soft at first but steady. As it grows in intensity I see one of the guards begin to act as if it has been called by someone. It nods to the other and hurries out the door. As it leaves, AP-12 moves to the communal area and begins to clean off the breakfast table.

The ground begins to shake in unusual, non-rhythmic palpitations, nearly knocking me off my feet. Then sirens begin to sound: loud, blaring, and mind numbing. I can barely hear myself think. Another powerful vibration comes and I can hear metal wrenching under its force. Was the facility going to hold up? I am not sure. Is this part of Avi's escape plan? Debris begins to fall. At any second a piece of debris could land on us. I doubt things can get much worse and suggest, "We need to get out of here". And then – amid the sirens and quaking – the lights go out.

CHAPTER FOUR
THE ESCAPE

The natural lighting beams through the windows overhead, our only source of luminescence. "Twigs! Zuri!" I shout. "I'm going to check on them. Enkidu, see if you can find a way out. If not, we'll need to find somewhere safe, maybe under the table." As if some omnipotent power with a sense of humor heard my words, the heavy, white air filtration unit above the communal area comes crashing down on top of the cafeteria table. Dust puffs up and floats in the air, thinning as it settles on the floor. Looking up, I see there is a hole left in the ceiling. "Maybe we can get out that way." I point upwards. "I'm going to get Twigs and Zuri. Enkidu, see if you can figure out a way up."

"Sure, no problem," he mumbles, dusting himself off.

Running to Twig's room, I see he is still under the covers of his bed and asleep. I step over to him and pull the covers back, revealing a pillow. Twigs is not here. He certainly picked a terrible time to disappear. With no idea where he might be, I sigh and make my way to Zuri's room.

She remains atop her bed: unmoving, undisturbed, and still in the wedding dress. Her chest rises and falls, a slow and steady sign that she's okay, for now. If I can't find some way to undo her coma… A crash sounds behind me, one of clanking metal, and it echoes. Looking towards the source of the sound I realize it was the stairway leading up to the second level. Some of the other railing has detached overhead. If Zuri and I don't get out soon, then it could fall and pin us in.

Grabbing her by the shoulders and shaking, I hope it will warrant some reaction. I'm certainly not strong enough to carry her out of here. Another tremor comes, strong enough to knock me off my feet. Standing back up, I move over to her and shout, "Zuri, if you can hear me. We are in danger. We need to leave, now!"

In a blink of an eye, her hand is on my throat, shooting up too quickly for me to react. She throws me back and my head smashes into the wall. I am seeing stars when I feel the burst of energy explode from her.

Coming to my senses, I look up, and to my utter amazement, see electricity sparking out all around her. I struggle to my feet and can feel a warm wetness matting my hair to the back of my head. Gazing upon Zuri, her eyes are open…but they are different, completely white with no iris or pupil to be seen. Her skin is glowing, not a warm yellow but a dark purple. It reminds me of a black light. It is as if the blood under her skin is lighting up her whole body, a similar glow to the one I take on while I hold Artemis, only darker. Her hair is flailing wildly and has turned completely white. She's floating, hovering with her feet a few inches above the ground, and staring daggers through me.

"Where is Prefect Gray?"

Her voice sounds terrible, like three different ones combined, all feminine and powerful. She doesn't even have to shout to be heard over the blare of the siren.

Gasping for breath, I reply. "I'm not sure where Prefect Gray is. Zuri, are you okay?" Electricity continues to spark from her body and I can feel it in the air. The hairs on the back of my neck stand up and I feel pangs, like needles digging into my skin.

She demands once more, "Where is Prefect Gray?"

I repeat, "Zuri, I don't know. Please, calm down. We've got to get out of here. Zuri, please..."

She interjects. "Zuri? Zuri — is dead." Lifting her finger, she points at me and a bolt of electricity sends me flying back against the wall again, this time wood crunching and softening the blow. For a few seconds the world is fuzzy and dark. Returning to reality, I see pieces of a guitar beneath me, scattered across the floor.

When I crawl out of the room, I see Enkidu hiding behind the fallen air purifier and Zuri...no, not Zuri... whatever she has become, nearing the door to the ward. Each crackle of electricity sounds like thunder and I can smell the burnt air. Not even bothering to look at her target, she points and a bolt shoots from her fingertip into the air purifier. Enkidu jumps away in time to avoid the full force of the resulting explosion but it still sends him flying. He lands with a thud and slides across the floor.

Two guards burst through the door before she reaches it and draw their guns, pointing at her. She laughs and sends lightning bolts into each of them. In a matter of seconds they are smoking and sparking on the ground and she is nearly out the door. I doubt there are enough guards in the facility to suppress her advance.

I am about to follow her out when I feel Enkidu's hand holding my shoulder. "You can't save them, not Lazarus nor Zuri. They are both beyond our reach. If you follow after her now, you'll only end up getting hurt...or worse...killed."

I watch the terrifying, white, floating figure on her way out of the ward. Suddenly, she sends two bursts of energy. The first is exactly in my direction. Inch by inch it sails toward me and I know I won't be able to react. A heavy thud pushes me out of the way and I turn to see AP-12.

The burst lands squarely in the middle of AP-12's chest, knocking him to his back. One by one his circuits blow, setting off a series of miniature explosions.

"Amy," he says, reaching up his hand toward me as the life leaves his robotic eyes and they go black.

The witch's second burst of energy is smaller and directed at the door's control panel. It fizzles for a second, just as she reaches the hallway, and then pops. The door slams shut behind her, trapping us inside. My heart breaks for AP-12. He saved my life.

My sadness is shattered by a terrifying roar that reverberates throughout the facility. It is so loud and jarring that I cover my ears until it ends. My heart jumps and my senses become more aware. Fear in me overtakes the pain in my body and my preoccupation for Zuri is forgotten. "What on earth was that?" I ask.

"I don't know," Enkidu answers. I can barely hear him over the sirens. For the first time since I'd met him he appears legitimately terrified. "But whatever it is...it sounds angry."

I can't help but worry about Twigs, Lazarus, Zuri, and how we're going to get out of this. The quaking continues and piece by piece our world is falling apart around us.

I know we can't give up. Falling debris and the shaking earth let me know we don't have much time left.

Remembering the thing I'd seen outside, I shudder. What if it decides to come back? We'd be defenseless and trapped. What if

Enkidu was right and we had moved to somewhere else? There is no telling where we are. Even if we get outside what are our chances of survival?

Seconds appear to be hours as we fight to find a way out, searching for an air vent and trying to build a ladder out of the broken stairway. Each effort is met with failure.

Artemis suggests, "Try to use your magic!"

"What?" I ask, confused.

"Use me to amplify your power," she explains, "so you can blast away the door!"

Stepping over to the door, I place Artemis's necklace around my head, and, reaching out the other, I close my eyes and focus my energy. A strange tingling flows from one hand to the other, passing through the very core of my body. As the sensation reaches my fingertips a burst of energy shoots forth, sending an arrow of light whizzing toward the door, exploding upon impact.

"Whoa!" Enkidu exclaims.

As the dust settles we realize the door is left unscathed, electric sparks dancing across its surface. "I couldn't do it," I mutter, hanging my head. "It didn't work."

"It was your first try," Artemis encourages. "Try again! Quick!"

Unchecked fires are spreading now, along the walls of our ward and throughout some of the living areas, pulling oxygen from the air and making it more difficult to breathe. Smoke is filling the air.

My vision is beginning to dim when the ward door blows open on its own accord. Startled, peering through the smoke, I watch as Avi comes into the room, holding one of the guns I've seen the guards use. Breathing heavily and outwardly terrified, he scans the room until he finds us and holsters his weapon.

"You're alive, thank god. If you follow me, I can get us out safely. The creature is merciless and it is only a matter of time until it makes its way here!" Avi shouts.

"It?" I yell back. "What is happening?"

"A monster is attacking the facility, tearing it to pieces and killing everything it sees. We can't let it find us. You can't even imagine the destruction it's already caused. I've never seen anything like it. No time for details but..."

I interrupt. "Where is my brother? Is he okay? You said you would try to save him!"

"Lazarus... is lost." He pauses.

Tears begin to fill in my eyes, making my vision blurry.

"I am so sorry, Amy." He pauses, walks over to me and places his hand on my arm. "But we need to go."

"What about the Ais?" Enkidu questions, adding, "And Twigs has disappeared. We don't know where he is."

"I'm right here," a voice sounds behind me. I turn to see Twigs, my heart wishing it was Lazarus instead.

Avi exclaims, "There's no time to get the Ais".

Defiant and wiping the tears from my face, I say, "I'm not leaving without them".

One of Avi's white guards joins us. "Sir, there isn't much more time. Preparations have been made for our escape. I have loaded the food rations as you ordered."

Avi introduces the guard. "This is Syd, my most trusted companion and dear friend. I've never met anyone who is a better shot. Amy, I'll go get the Ais. You, Twigs, and Enkidu go with Syd."

I direct my words to Avi. "I'm going with you to get the Ais. It would be crazy for you to go alone in this current situation."

"If Amy is going, then so am I," Enkidu says.

"Me too!" Twigs shouts.

"Fine." Avi gives in to our demand.

Avi leads us down the hall, hustling us along, avoiding debris and turning down different hallways until we come to a lab. In the distance we hear another roar, followed by the sounds of screams and running footsteps.

Catching my breath and looking around, I can only imagine what the lab we are in used to look like. Now it is a mangled mesh of metal, steel rods and sparking wires. Avi runs to a cabinet by the door and pulls out three canvas bags, handing one to each of us. "Against that wall." Avi points to the right. "Gather as many of those objects as you can." The wall is covered in a variety of jewelry: necklaces, bracelets, earrings, and rings. An occasional painting or piece of art is amongst them.

Rushing over, we begin to take things from the wall and place them in the bags. Each Ai takes on a different kind of glow as I touch it: blue, yellow, red, green, purple, and white. Gently I place them in my bag. Each time I hear a whispered, "Thank you". With the sirens I can't tell if the voice I hear is true or imagined but I choose to believe the former.

I look at Twigs, Avi, Enkidu, and Syd. The wall which held the Ais is now bare, every Ai safely loaded into our bags, with the exception of one, a stained glass painting which Twigs is holding in his hand.

He turns, tripping over a fallen cabinet. Somehow he's able to keep his balance but the glass slips through his fingers and crashes against the floor, splitting into thousands of shards. A scream of anguish which would rival any banshee's emerges from the shards as red light pillars up from the debris, taking on the form of a human.

The luminescent being faces Twigs, black holes taking the place of eyes and its mouth. Continuing its anguished wail, it lunges at a frightened Twigs, passing through him without causing any perceivable harm. Then it disintegrates into nothingness.

Unsure of what to make of the occurrence, I almost forget the situation we're in. Everyone is transfixed by the strange event. Avi is the one that brings our attention back. "Alright, let's go! This way!" We follow through more wreckage and unfamiliar halls.

"What happened back there?" Enkidu shouts, as he tries to keep up with Avi. I assume he is referring to the broken Ai.

Avi mumbles while leading us through the collapsing infrastructure, "When the reciprocal of an Ai is destroyed, it sends the Ai to Apollyon. I'll explain it all later. For now let's keep moving."

Eventually we reach a broken stairwell. "We have to go down that?" Twigs asks, his eyes wide as saucers.

Syd interjects. "There is no other way down, unless you care to take your chances by jumping out the window." Based on the steps below us, I estimate us to be nine or ten floors up. That would be ninety to a hundred feet. Depending on the terrain below, jumping might not be a bad idea. But I decide to keep this opinion to myself.

We struggle down the steps, jumping over crevices in the broken metal as we come to them. Some are over three feet in length. Twigs is unwilling to go on his own, so Syd is forced to carry him on his back and does so with little exertion. We go down five floors. I count them on the way. We haven't heard the roar of the monster for some time. I take it to be a good sign. Maybe the thing is long gone by now and we have escaped its wrath.

We come to a landing and exit the stairwell, running across what appears to be an office space. We reach the windows on the other side of the room. "Now we jump out the window," Avi declares. Glancing out, I see we are around fifty feet up. However, that isn't what shocks me. Looking out, all I can see is nothing but rolling sand dunes in every direction. Enkidu was right. We were moving the entire time.

"Isn't there another stairwell?" Twigs asks, jarring my focus back from my astonishment.

"It is too damaged to use. Who is going first?" Through the window opening, I can hear the wind howling and see the sand blowing.

"I'll go," I reply, climbing through the opening and sitting on its edge. I notice the sun setting in the distance, turning the sky a crimson. It seems appropriately symbolic for the events of the day... for all the bloodshed. Where are we? But before I can second guess what I'm doing, I am pushed off the ledge and brace myself for the landing.

Hitting the incline of a dune, I can't help but roll down, and it seems to have softened the initial impact of the fall. Still, my bare forearms are cut by stray grains of sand. I look to evaluate the damage only to see the skin around the wounds is rapidly closing. In mere seconds they are completely healed.

Enkidu comes next, shouting as he falls. He rolls and comes to a stop with a grunt and spitting a mouth full of sand out with a nauseating hack.

It is a strange feeling to be outside the building, in fresh air. Wind blowing against me and the warmth of the setting sun makes me feel alive again. But it doesn't last long, as I remember all the sacrifices that were made for us to finally be free. I shout over to Enkidu, "Once everyone is down, we'll want to leave ASAP and get as far away from this place as possible".

"No need to tell me twice," Enkidu agrees, still brushing sand out of his mouth.

Twigs is next but instead of jumping on his own accord, he appears to be thrown out of the window. I wonder if it is Avi or Syd who did the throwing. Avi jumps next and then Syd. The next series of events happens so fast. As Syd is falling, an explosion from the window throws him in the air and he lands awkwardly on his ankle. The building could take no more and begins to collapse in front of us, emitting a shockwave which sends us all flying in different directions.

Lying on my belly, I lift my head up and wipe the sand from my face. I hear a bellowing growl above me, like rolling thunder. Paralyzed in fear and pain, I hear it roar...the same earsplitting sound as before. Only it is much worse, penetrating every part of my body. I feel it as much as I hear it.

My nostrils begin to fill with the stench of death and blood as I feel the creature's warm breath against my skin. Drops of saliva fall next to me, soaking into the sand and creating moisture on my skin.

Knowing I am about to die, I turn over to see what is about to kill me. Opening my eyes, I am not prepared for what I witness. The largest and most terrifying worm I've ever seen stares back at me with no identifiable eyes: at least twenty five feet in diameter and as long as a football field. Long tusk-like teeth protrude from its mouth, still dripping saliva. Even without eyes, it seems to be examining me. Its powerful setae wriggle with anticipation and pull it closer to me. Inching closer, its horridness is magnified and I hope my impending death comes sooner rather than later. Terrified and overloaded, my head feels light. My senses overwhelmed and no longer able to withstand the shock, I black out.

....

Her emotions overcoming her, she begins to shake and cry. Unsure of how she will react, I put my arm around her shoulder to comfort her and she leans into me. I hold her in my arms; we don't say anything. We just cry and watch the suns rise, turning the dusky, pink sky into a brilliant, clear sapphire. Wispy cirrus clouds hold place high in the sky. The impressive mountains contrast with the smooth dunes. Sitting there in silence the tears eventually pass...but we both know the sadness of loss never will.

....

ACT TWO
THE FATHER

CHAPTER ONE
GENESIS

Looking out into the auditorium, I don't see an empty seat. In the dim light, it is difficult to recognize any distinguishable details of the people sitting in the balcony. On the floor level, men and women wear their best attire: suits, tuxedos, and evening gowns.

The men's modern tuxedos and suits sport a ruffled design on the shoulders and arms. Pinstripes accent the ruffles and turn into straight lines down the forearms and around the center of the suit, both front and back. Their bowties are a stiff fabric, forming triangles which face downward, their bottom point folded back behind. Many of them have matching leather gloves. Some of the women are dressed in similar suits, whereas others wear gowns with sharp edges, bright colors, and varying designs: some traditional and others modern.

I can recognize some of the people, each an expert in their respective field of science. Some were my idols when I was growing up. Knowing it will be my turn to speak soon is humbling, to say the least.

The woman at the podium finishes her presentation and sits down to my right. Clapping from the crowd echoes throughout the room. A man on my left stands and takes her place at the podium. He begins, "The person you are about to hear needs no introduction. Over the past fifteen years his inventions have impacted all of humanity, forever altering Earth's course. The potential application of his most recent technology has generated much excitement. And discussion. He is here to talk about the future of his nanotechnology and its potential applications. With no further ado, I present to you Dr. Avi Taylor."

I stand, passing the man as he returns to his seat, and take my place in front of the audience. I am met with applause, a few dirty looks, and many curious expressions. Public speaking has never been something I enjoy, especially when there is adversity inherent in the topic. "Thank you for your introduction," I begin. "Thank you all for coming this evening. Nanotechnology and related fields have exponentially changed over the last thirty years. What once seemed impossible has become a reality." I nervously pause, trying to maintain my composure. If anyone else could have presented in my place I would have allowed them to. Nonetheless, I am the expert, the only one qualified to answer all the questions which are sure to come.

I continue. "I am, of course, aware of the sensitive issues which have been in the media as of late. If I did not believe in the life changing, positive influence of our picobots, I would not be here today. Our picobots are one trillionth of a meter in diameter, six to eight million times smaller than a red blood cell. Their size allows them to travel through the bloodstream unabated, targeting mutated cells, harmful viruses, and negative bacteria: manipulating such malignancies on an atomic level. We are able to program these picobots to our liking, and by so doing we have effectively rid the world of cancer and many other illnesses. Today we'd like to speak with you about the promising future of this technology."

A woman in the front row interrupts the presentation. "What about the rumors of the terrorist organizations right here at home? Last week one of them took credit for the annihilation of Albin, Wyoming, a small town here in the United States."

She continues unchallenged. A few stir in their seats uncomfortably. "Certain terrorist groups say they have developed WMD's implementing similar technology to yours, capable of erasing an entire city. Can you explain why someone can't continue to misuse your technology?"

"I understand your concerns but we are going to stay on topic with today's presentation," I deflect and try to continue.

Another audience member shouts, "Stay on topic? What happened last week in Albin had the world's attention. This IS your topic!"

Security guards start to make their way down the auditorium's passages. I direct my answer to the outburst. "Most of our discoveries are open sourced, allowing other companies to use and improve upon what we have already developed. Knowing this, we implemented certain protocols, to prevent as much misuse as we could."

The man asks, "Do you have any other safeguards to keep things from getting out of hand? It is quite clear with recent events that your protocols can be overridden too easily."

"In our own institutions," I answer, "each individual nanobot and picobot receives a signal from a control beacon. Those who wish to use their own picobots are required to implement similar beacons. Taylor Industries is allowed to evaluate said constructs on a semi-annual basis as per the license. These beacons control all of the bots and we can remotely access any beacon from any agency. In other words, we have control over each individual machine created by us or by other organizations. That is how we can best protect everyone from the misuse of this technology."

Taking a deep breath, I add, "Even so, the terrorist groups you refer to may be utilizing nanotechnology in their weapons, a field of science we developed thirty years ago. The progress of methodical and systematic studies and developments is inevitable. I cannot halt the progress of every other scientist. I feel the best way to survive attacks, like the ones you have been hearing about in the news, is to develop defense systems which nullify the effects of the WMD's."

A man asks, "Are you saying you have a way to defend against picotech driven WMD's?"

I reply, "Transient electromagnetic disturbances have naturally occurred since the dawn of time. A directed energy weapon can replicate these disturbances through radiation, radio frequencies, and microwaves. DEW's have existed for years and would be more than sufficient to defend against any mechanized weapon, regardless of said weapon's size and make up."

The gentleman continues to prod. "Are you saying that a simple electromagnetic pulse is enough to prevent Eric Drexler's gray goo scenario?"

"Essentially," I answer, "Drexler's gray goo scenario has always been hypothetical. Even if robots were somehow able to glitch and reprogram themselves to replicate, using everything they come across as material: buildings, cars, houses, and even biological material, they wouldn't be defenseless against an energy pulse.

"At Taylor Industries we have already implemented a safety protocol which utilizes an EMP to supplement the control beacons. Similarly, we require all shared technology institutions to utilize the same contingency. As rumors of weaponization have grown, and as the possibility of the future weaponization of nanotech becomes more likely, we have begun to work on a focused, portable version of our EMP beacons. We see it as our moral obligation. Now, if we can return to the presentation..."

A woman joins the interrogation. "Within the past few years we have finally reached the point of singularity, artificial intelligence has matched and is surpassing human intelligence as we speak. Even in your own company it is the robots who are innovating — not us. We have taken their place as assistants. It has been said the only way for humanity to survive is to merge with the more intelligent technology. Some people already have artificial organs and their minds have been enhanced by computers.

"You say you can control your technology. Eventually, the exponential growth of things will find a way around EMP's and control beacons. How do you guarantee there will always be a safety contingency in place to regulate potentially dangerous uses of this technology?"

Security guards reach the woman and begin to motion for her to leave.

"That won't be necessary," I state, looking at the security guards. Her question is the one which is on everyone's mind and it is the question I have been fearing. Breathing deeply, I answer, "There is no way to guarantee a safety contingency will always be in place. Everyone on Earth is an individual with the ability to make their own choices. With those choices come consequences. Ultimately, humanity will be left to decide its own fate. We cannot un-invent guns or atomic weapons. This technology is no different. There is no turning back." The room begins to break out in angered shouting and I realize the presentation is over. "Thank you for your time," I say, retreating from the podium.

I exit backstage as guards begin to escort people from the auditorium. An announcement comes over the loudspeaker, asking people to please remain calm.

My bodyguards, Syd and Alex, approach me from behind. With the increased fear of what my technology could do to humanity and the planet, there has been more than one attempt on my life, and Syd and Alex have become an unfortunate necessity. Both of them wear black suits with matching gloves. Alex has his long, blond hair slicked back and tied into a pony tail. Protective transition lens glasses cover his dark blue eyes. Though I am of average height, Alex is a full head taller. His build would have allowed him to pursue a career as a professional wrestler, had he so chosen.

Syd is a redhead, slightly shorter than Alex but of a similar build and slightly more athletic. He was an Olympic caliber decathlon athlete prior to his employment as my Executive Security Officer. His green eyes are left uncovered.

Syd remarks, "That wasn't so bad. No one threw anything at you this time."

"No, but they probably would have without the security checks when they came in," I answer. "All I wanted to do was make the world a better place. But they say the road to hell is paved in good intentions, right? Do you think my critics are right? Am I bringing the planet closer to its destruction with what I've created?"

"Maybe," Syd answers, patting me on the back. "But there's not much to be done for that, now. All you can do is continue to make the world a better place. You can do things no one else can. Just keep on keeping on."

"I suppose. Let's get to the banquet," I sigh and force a smile. Not a fan of menial interactions with people who I've never seen before, I never looked forward to social events. "Maybe if I'd focused my efforts on cloning I'd be able to send a doppelgänger in my place."

"That would be no good, sir," Syd says. "If you had focused on cloning you wouldn't have made so many enemies and you'd have no need for me. I'd be out of a job."

Recognizing his dry sense of humor, I play into his joke. "Are you valuing your employment over our lives?"

"What can I say, sir? I'm selfish."

We both chuckle. Alex remains stoic, unmoving and staring straight ahead. I pat his shoulder and tell him, "Lighten up. Everyone has left now, no need to keep up the scary stay away or else image."

"Sorry, sir," he replies and his shoulders relax. Alex has always been uptight and hyper alert. It makes him a great bodyguard but a poor conversationalist.

Syd says, "The limo is waiting for us out back. I am ready to go when you are."

"Thank you," I tell him.

We walk further backstage and open the exit door which leads to the alley. Stepping outside, a brisk evening air blows against my skin and I slip into the limo. Its motor roars into life and we are on our way to the White and Gold Gala, a charity event whose proceeds sponsor scholarships for children interested in scientific studies. Various assemblies and presentations, like the one I just participated in, were scheduled all over town as a precursor to the annual event.

I gaze out the window, marveling at how much things have changed in the last twenty years. What we used to consider artificial intelligence was anything but intelligent. Recently it has evolved to fit its name. Cars drive themselves, including our limo. Buildings, houses, traffic lights, televisions, and phones are all controlled by AI: guiding people through from day to day.

Even the buildings look different, now. The ones outside are painted in various colors, from pastel to fluorescent. They have rounded edges and roofs. Some of the taller structures are connected near the top by a highly resistant, lightweight, plastic tubing. It allows people to traverse from one edifice to the other with ease, while at the same time providing a base of structural integrity in the constructs. Some of the buildings are wider, supporting entire communities within: different levels being dedicated to childcare, shopping, and living.

Cement in the sidewalks and asphalt in the streets have been infused with a bacteria which reacts to the elements, allowing them to repair themselves when they crack. The AI in vehicles has made traffic lights a thing of the past. Mathematical equations and speed adjustments allow vehicles to shoot through intersections without incident.

Holographic advertisements hover in the air between buildings, personalized for the person who sees them. Where I see an advertisement for a new pair of dress shoes, Alex might see hunting boots.

Though the world has gone through a metamorphosis, the initiatives and hopes of people rarely change. We desire the same things people did two thousand years ago: security, purpose, and love. The third is something I am yet to find, never having been part of a true family.

I justify this fact, telling myself family has become less important in today's society. People focus on achievements and personal advancements and less on leaving behind a living legacy, especially now that most diseases have been eradicated and the current estimation of human life expectancy is to surpass one-hundred and fifty years.

Nations have united into a world government, redefining currencies and social constructs. Upon reaching the singularity — when artificial intelligence passed the Turing Test and matched human intelligence — suffering was stifled and humanity was led into a brief period of peace and prosperity. It didn't last long, as the lack of natural selection led to overpopulation, a problem I aim to solve next.

The event hall comes into view up ahead, a white domed stadium used to host various activities ranging from local sporting events, high profile concerts, and other conventions. In recent months professional athletic competitions have all but halted, anti-technology terrorist groups seeing such activities as prime targets, especially since the event in Albin. For the gala tonight, extra measures have been made to assure everyone's safety. That is what I'm told, anyway.

As if reading my thoughts, Syd says, "It is safe. You don't need to worry. Even if someone managed to breach the defenses, they'd still have to get past Alex and me. We won't let anything happen to you."

"That's not what I'm worried about," I tell him. My true preoccupation comes from my social anxiety. "I'm concerned with having to make small talk. It's just something I'd rather not do."

"Sounds tough," he says, grinning ear to ear. "If worse comes to worse, we'll let Alex talk to them in your stead."

The thought makes me smile and I ask, "Is Alex capable of small talk while he's on the job?"

Alex shakes his head no.

"Ah, come on," Syd teases. "Take one for the team."

Alex replies, "Won't happen. It is my job to keep him safe from physical harm. His social anxieties are his problem or possibly his psychologist's."

"I don't have a psychologist," I pronounce.

"Maybe you should look into getting one," he says. Having worked with Alex for a few months, I know he's joking, but his serious tone takes some getting used to.

"How is your family?" I ask him. "Great," he says. "Once this public relations tour is over, I look forward to getting home with them."

"Just two more weeks," I say.

He smiles and nods.

The limousine comes to a stop next to the arena. Getting out, Alex and Syd position themselves on each side of me. Alert, they scan the area and we make our way to the gala. Modern interpretations of cultural dances from around the world provide most of the entertainment for the evening. Interacting with my colleagues, I find a former college roommate and we discuss his advances in the study of antigravity. Even as a scientist, astrophysics was always a branch of science that made my head spin. "The trick to interstellar travel isn't finding a wormhole," he explains. "The challenge is keeping the wormhole open once it's found. Antimatter is the key to achieving this."

"Even if you did find a wormhole and keep it open," I ask, "how would you know where it goes?"

"By looking to see what is on the other side," he tells me with a smile.

"I'm not going to be the one who signs up for that expedition," I declare.

He winks. "Come now, Dr. Taylor. Where is your sense of adventure?"

The conversation continues and leads to other topics: singularities, negative energy, and picotechnology. Around midnight things begin to wind down, people returning to their homes, and I signal to my guards it is time to do the same.

On the way out the door a short robot stops me: rolling directly into my path, looking at me with her binocular shaped eyes, and extending her hand, which holds a card. 'AP-11' is painted on the left half of her chest. She speaks with a slightly awkward Indian accent. "Dr. Taylor, it is so nice to meet you." The robot is careful to let me move towards her, knowing Syd and Alex will react to anything they perceive to be aggressive.

"AP-11," I reply, stepping closer, taking her card, and examining it. There is no organization written on its surface, just a phone number. "Was there something you needed?"

"Something of the utmost importance. My employer has a job proposal for you," the robot explains.

Making sure to remain polite, I explain, "I am sorry but maybe we could discuss this later". I hand the robot my own card. "It is awfully late and I have an early flight tomorrow."

AP-11 takes the card, saying, "Very well. We will be in contact with you, Dr. Taylor. Have a nice evening."

We work through the thinning crowd and exit the building. No more than three steps out the front door and things become a blur, Syd pulling me to the ground. Two gunshots ring out and I feel them whizz above my head. The assailant is no more than five feet away. It is a miracle he missed. Now Alex is on him: disarming the man, twisting his arm behind his back, and holding his cheek against the cold concrete.

Syd helps me back to my feet and ushers me into the limo. The door shuts and we begin to drive away. "Are you okay?" he asks, examining me from head to toe and ensuring I'm wound free.

"I am," I tell him, taking in a deep breath to calm my nerves. "But I'm ready to be back in the hotel. That is enough excitement for one night."

Sitting in a square office with a single oak desk in front of me, I wait. Syd and Alex stand behind me, one on each side. The room is perfectly organized, not an office supply out of place and not a spot on the beige carpet and walls. Trying to acquire an understanding of the office's owner, I search for clues about interests or places traveled. Where most would have souvenirs of the past, I see nothing but empty shelves. There is not a single picture on the wall. The only guest chair is the one I am in. Windows are open, letting in a midday sun, adding to the sense of emptiness associated with the room.

"Dr. Taylor," a robotic voice says, as the door to the hallway opens, "it is so nice to see you again. I am glad you decided to stay an extra day to meet with us."

"AP-11," I answer, "you and I both know I didn't decide to meet with you today. And we both understand you aren't going to let me go about my life until we discuss whatever it is you wanted to discuss. How did you manage to get my flight cancelled, anyway?"

Her head cocks to the side. It is almost like she is confused. "I didn't cancel your flight. My employer did. As to how they accomplished it, you will have to ask them."

"I plan to," I grumble. "Where are they?"

"Here," AP-11 replies, turning to face the blank, white wall. The window shades begin to close on their own, enveloping the room in darkness, and then AP-11's eyes flash, projecting an image onto the wall, one of a woman, whose bleach blonde hair is pulled tight into a bun behind her head.

Her eyes examine me for a few seconds and then she speaks. "Dr. Taylor, I am happy to finally meet you. My name is Prefect Gray. I am the director of our operations."

"To the point please." I force myself to remain calm.

She says, without regard to my comment, "Before we get into the details, I hear you had an encounter with an anti-tech rebel last night. In the coming months it won't be the last. You know as well as I that a war is brewing. Surely you've noticed?"

"Well, people are scared," I answer. "Our problems are the same ones we've faced over the last thirty years: an exploding population on Earth with limited resources. Our first artificial planet, New World I, has already met its population capacity and New World II will not be completed for another three years." I look her straight in the eyes. "War is not what we need to worry about. Sustainability is. Our food supply is our greatest challenge moving forward."

She stares back and listens, hollow eyes unblinking. "I agree," she insists.

"Average people don't realize how bad the situation has become. Fertile land to grow food to support the population is becoming increasingly difficult to maintain," I say. "We're hoping to resolve that problem before the public needs to know the severity of the situation. My studies show that we are on the brink of experiencing crop failure. Enough of this small talk, whatever you have going on here, I'm sorry but I don't have time to help with it. My focus and obligation is to humanity."

"Exactly," her mouth curls upward into an unnerving smile. "You and I share many of the same goals. You have been utilizing your pico-technology to modify food sources: grain, fruits, and vegetables. From what I have been told you are increasing the rate at which they grow by a full 400 percent, making it five times faster to grow and harvest a crop?"

"How did you know that?" I ask. "We haven't made that information public."

Who is she? First she has my flight cancelled and now she has confidential information from my company. The worst part of all this — I don't know anything about her. She says, "What matters is that we are essentially doing the same thing, just applied a little differently."

I protest. "I don't know how you got that information but I do know you are overstepping your bounds."

She hangs her head. "I'm sorry you feel that way."

"I won't be able to help you," I explain, standing to leave the room.

"Dr. Taylor," she stops me. "I don't think you understand what's going on here. An escort ship will pick you up in 24 hours. I'm afraid you don't have a choice. I will see you at our facility soon. Good day."

The image dissipates as the windows open and AP-11's eyes turn back to normal. The robot shifts her head so she is looking at me and blinks. "You are free to leave."

"What do you mean it was empty?" I ask the police officer, whose last name, Ruiz, is embroidered in yellow letters on the upper right side of his blue uniform.

Sitting across from me on the other side of the desk, he replies, "We went to the building and the room you described was empty, not even a desk or chair. The phone number you provided us is disconnected and it has never been registered to anyone. We name checked the individual you mentioned too. Nothing. I'm not sure what you are playing at, but we don't appreciate it. Chasing ghosts is a waste of our time."

"She's real," I insist, wondering what happens next. If the police can't help me, who can?

That evening I am on my back, resting in a field of green near my country home and gazing up at the stars. They are impossible to see from within the city: Orion, the Big Dipper, and Cassiopeia overhead. New World I, a manmade and terraformed mini-planet, shines brighter than the moon in the midnight sky. It stands as a symbol of the first human-AI partnership and has functioned to complement our natural world in supporting the ever-increasing population.

The Life Bridge connects New World II to our planet, similar to what was in place when they built New World I. The tube has a diameter of 500 miles and is used to exchange resources back and forth. Special spheres can be used to transport people. Aside from conveyance, the Life Bridge holds New World II in place, preventing it from succumbing to gravity and falling out of space while it is being built.

My two-wing mansion is in the lush countryside, isolated from neighbors and any unwanted human interactions. A gate around it and automated security system assure no unwelcome guests stop by for a visit. A long driveway leads from the main gate to the front door.

Examining the sky, I reflect on my encounter with the strange woman, thinking maybe I'd gone crazy, but Syd and Alex insist it wasn't imagined.

What is she doing with my research? Who is she? If I'm going to have any chance at surviving my encounter with this mysterious woman, I need to understand who she is and what motivates her. Maybe this is just some kind of a joke?

My secretary and assistants have played jokes on me before but nothing like this. How could they get my flight cancelled and where would they find a robot like AP-11?

If it isn't a joke, what are these people working on? What obstacle have they come across? Why do they need me to help them overcome it? How did they get access to my technology without me knowing about it in the first place? Whoever these people are, they are powerful, and perhaps dangerous. It looks like I have no choice if this is all true. The only thing I can do is run.

I sit up, roll up my sleeve and tell my wrist communicator to call Syd. It obeys and when he answers his image is displayed and magnified from the small screen, creating a projection which hovers over my wrist.

"What is the plan?" he asks.

"Pack your bags and get a hold of Alex so he does the same," I tell him. "It is time for us to get out of Dodge, time to disappear."

The sun rises the next morning, melting the morning mist and evaporating dew from the grass. I see my limo approaching and move to the driveway to meet it. It stops next to me and the door opens, allowing me to see Syd and Alex inside. Lifting my suitcase, I toss it in the trunk before finding my place next to Syd.

The door closes and the limo's engine hums to life as it begins to move forward. Syd asks, "When is the last time you've been to the cabin?"

"Years," I reply. "If it is this woman's intent to take me by force, she will have to find me. Considering you two didn't know about the cabin until this morning, we should be safe there. I needed a vacation, anyway."

We arrive at the cabin four hours later, exactly twenty three hours after my conversation with the woman. The cabin is situated on the edge of a lake in the middle of the Rocky Mountains.

Standing at the water's edge, Syd, Alex, and I skip rocks across the calm surface and wonder about the woman. "What happens if you do see her again?" Syd asks.

"She will find us, I am sure of it," I reply. "I brought you both here to buy us some time. I would never ask you to come and do this with me."

"Nonsense!" shouts Syd. "We're in this together."

"Agreed," Alex states.

I smile. Pride swells inside me. "Well, since we are here killing time, who is up for some fishing while we wait for our kidnappers?" I smirk.

Alex says, "I thought you'd never ask".

We spend the next hour fishing. Wind whistles in the reeds, crickets chirp, and the fluctuating current of the lake creates a gentle crash, completing nature's calming orchestra. It is strange how being so far away from the modern world can help someone understand the natural one.

It is this calming separation from humanity's advancements and technology which makes a sound in the distance appear so foreign. It starts as a metallic hum. Then it grows, becoming something similar to an approaching aircraft. A black dot accompanies the sound. As it gets closer I recognize it as a custom model of hovercopter.

Its black surface shines in the cloudless sky, reflecting sunlight. The object floats through the sky like an agile bee and its shape is oddly similar to said insect. Blue engines glow as it stops overhead and their intensity diminishes as the craft begins to lower and I realize, she's found me. This isn't a joke.

The craft touches down between the lake and the cabin, a walkway extending at an angle to the ground as the door opens and AP-11 begins her descent. She rumbles over loose gravel, dirt, grass, and sagebrush until she's next to me. She asks, "Dr. Taylor, have you made your decision? We would love to work with you." Looking behind her, I see four black-clad and armed individuals waiting inside the vehicle.

Recognizing how trapped I am, I know I am left with one ploy — to go along with AP-11. I tell her, "I have".

"Good," she says touching a button activating a communicator on her arm, which projects a holographic image of the woman's face.

She says, "I am happy to see you again. Beautiful place you have here."

It almost feels like making a deal with the devil. "I'd like to see your facility and more fully understand the research you are doing," I tell her. "I'll go willingly."

"This is a pleasant surprise," she beams. "From our understanding, you prefer to travel with your two guards. They will be coming with you, yes?" "Yes." I can't believe I am agreeing to this. What other choice do I have? If I don't go along with her then the armed guards will just drag me away.

"Very well. There are spots for you and your guards on the craft. From there, you will be brought to our research facility where we will finally meet in person. I will see you in a few hours."

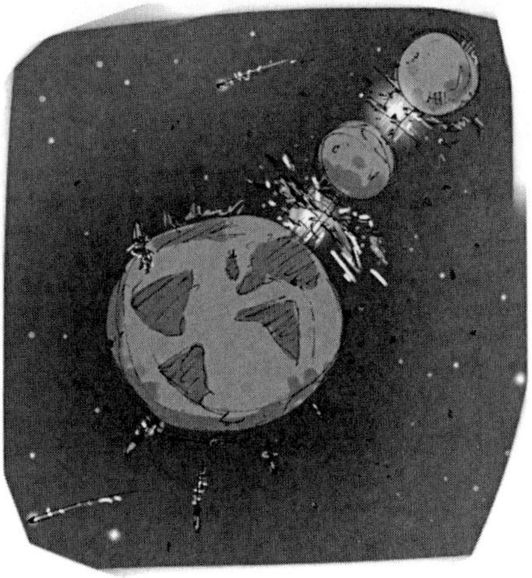

CHAPTER TWO
EXODUS

A few hours later I am in the back of yet another limo, heading north, Alex to my left and Syd to my right. AP-11 is in front of us against a wall. Outside the window there is dead yellow grass covering hills on each side of the interstate. We pass the occasional remnants of oil pumps, decaying relics. Oil hasn't been used as a source of energy in well over two decades. In the west there is a mountain range on the horizon.

AP-11 hands me a tablet with new documents and I evaluate them one at a time and review the information they contain. "We've made great progress," she explains. "What we've achieved is an enhancement of the human efficiency, allowing our test subjects to instantaneously heal from minor scrapes and cuts, and comprehend their surroundings at a seemingly psychic level. They deduce things which normal humans can't and can eat less food and get more out of it. They also tend to be more athletic and need less sleep."

I begin to look over the information she's passed to me. While I read, AP-11 begins to slide something out from below her seat. I realize it is yarn and crochet hooks. Picking up a half-made sweater, she sets it on her lap and crochets. A few years back I might have been surprised by the sight but robots have become humanlike in many respects. Knowing I should focus on the task at hand, I turn my attention back to the tablet.

It is hard for me to keep my emotions in check when I realize they've been using my research in pico-technology and applying it to humans. Names flash across the screen: Habbicus, Zuri, Amy, Gable, Olivia, and Doug. It surprises me to see Gable on the list, the multi-millionaire who vanished recently. The media still hasn't stopped covering the story, theorizing about what might have happened to cause the disappearance. Most people believing that he sought a more simple life.

The others are equally intriguing. Habbicus is a child genius who received most of his education through homeschooling. He graduated from his advanced high school level curriculum at the age of nine and would have been going on to the university before his involvement with Prefect Gray's project. Examining his picture, I notice hollow eyes, not an ounce of emotion in them.

Zuri's file reports she was recently married, a young woman in her late twenties, and a talented musician. She directed music for her city's local symphony and had even composed some of her own work. It indicates she was raised in a lower class family and was close to her parents.

Olivia was a local small business owner. Apparently she was known for her astuteness, attention to detail, and her quick wit.

Doug was a university student whose aptitude with computers and high grades in school earned him a scholarship to any college of his choice. While attending school, he earned a name for himself as a competitive gamer, recognized on a world level for his aptitude.

Amy is Doug's twin sister. They are both from a large family, and multi-talented. Unlike the others, she didn't excel in any single arena but she seemed to be very good at a lot of things: athletics, academics, and social interactions.

AP-11 interrupts my reading. "We are nearing the facility and will be arriving shortly."

Peering out the window, I notice we are nearing a town. It seems relatively small, with mostly residential areas along the highway. I see an air force base to the left with three white, long-range missiles by its front gate. They are lined up in a row, straight up and down, relics of a bygone age. A few seconds later, a high school and football field are on the right. The end zones read Central High School in faded red letters on a worn black background.

We continue past the city farther into the prairie. I can see a tall cylindrical tower appearing in the distance. We take the next exit and begin down a road leading to the complex. We pass through a gate and park next to it. I realize how truly massive this place is.

AP-11 opens up a compartment in her chest and places her yarn and hooks inside. Getting out of the vehicle, we get a better look at the structure. It is constructed with a white metal alloy and painted gold around the windows and doors. Its cylindrical design is topped with a golden dome, resembling those of a capital building. The base of the edifice is at least two hundred yards in diameter.

"Here we are," AP-11 chimes. "Our building is constructed of carbon fiber and duranium." She begins tapping an icon on her black wrist band and opens the front door. The building is mostly empty, probably because it is an early Saturday morning. The ground level is a wide hall with three towering modern marble statues to the right, a water feature, bamboo shoots, and a reception desk straight ahead. We continue towards a set of large stairs near the back.

"We will head upstairs to meet with Prefect Gray. I am sure she is anxious to finally meet you in person." We continue to follow AP-11 to the stairwell. We arrive on the next floor. It looks like an empty call center or collection agency, lots of small cubical spaces, each with their own computer and phone. Walking parallel to the west wall, we move to the next corner and up another flight of steps.

Arriving at the third floor, the stairs stop abruptly at a solid white panel, completely bare aside from a biometrics scanner. Two security cameras are attached on each side of the wall. AP-11 touches her wristband and the scanner turns on. Pressing her hand firmly against it, the panel slides opens. We step through and I notice the strange thickness of the walls.

Just inside, I see Prefect Gray approach us, extending her hand. "A pleasure to finally meet you," she bellows. "I do hope your journey was pleasant."

I shake her hand and carefully choose my words. "Indeed. Your robot gave me an interesting look at what you have been working on here."

"It is very exciting," she confirms. "Let me show you what this place is. It will be easier than telling you. This is the security floor," she explains. "We test our guards here, all of them robots with special enhancements to their AI. We also develop and test new weapon technology on this floor."

I raise an eyebrow and question, "You have your own weapon technology? Isn't that a little excessive?"

"Oh, heavens no. You'll see why this is required soon enough," she contests. The area is a furniture-free rectangle with four chambers, one in each corner. The walls are made up of white panels. There are padded mats on the floor and countless guards in black armor moving around. They are testing unfamiliar projectile weapons, using holograms as their targets. Lockers line all four walls at varying intervals.

"What else can you tell me about these guns?" Syd questions. "I've never seen anything like them before."

She replies, "They are plasma-based weapons. They are currently set on low levels of energy for training purposes but one full energy blast contains enough power to down an elephant or even something much larger."

"Why would you need to something so powerful?" I push.

"Because," she replies, "there are things which are much bigger and scarier than elephants." She smirks, and, moving to a far wall, she pauses and opens two of the lockers.

"I have taken the liberty of making a special white armor for your two guards. It will help them stand out from the others and you will be able to tell them apart with little effort," she says, holding the uniforms out to Alex and Syd. They take the uniforms in their arms and then look at me, untrusting expressions on their faces. Noticing the hesitation, Prefect Gray adds, "As I said before, we are all on the same team".

Syd interlocks the fingers of his hands and lets them hang in front of him, his thumb tapping, and he asks, "What do we need armored uniforms for?" It takes me a few seconds to realize it but the question is a cover for what he really wants to say. The rhythmic tapping of his thumb is Morse code. He asks me, "Can we trust her?"

I lift my hand to my face and feign to scratch an itch on my temple before tapping a quick reply — "No option".

"Let me show you." She proceeds into the next room and we follow, Syd and Alex carrying their uniforms in their arms. AP-11 trails behind.

The next room has glass cases along the walls, layered one on top of the other in sets of two and three, depending on the size of each one. Creatures I have never seen before are inside each of them: large rodents, strange worms, and beetle-like insects. I see an animal which is a mixture between a mouse and a rabbit, with a small glowing orb between the ears, no bigger than a medium-sized dog.

"What are these? Where did you get them?" I ask in amazement.

"We brought them here from a planet called Mythe," she explains. "It is an alien world we have been exploring over the past year using our technological advances. It is a very interesting place — far more dangerous than we had ever imagined. The ecosystem there is incredibly sophisticated. That is why we need the weapons and armor."

"You..." I begin, pausing to grasp what I am hearing, "you found evidence of life outside our own?"

"You're looking at it, Dr. Avi," Prefect Gray responds, grinning.

We follow Prefect Gray out of the room and to an elevator, ascending to another floor. AP-11 remains in the chamber with the strange animals. Stepping into a hall, she spins an entire 360 degrees, raising her arms over her head and telling us, "And this...this is where the magic happens". The floor is made from a marble and slate checkered tile. It seems unnecessary and overly expensive for a research facility, even one housing alien animals.

Artificial environment control vents are overhead, helping maintain a comfortable temperature and humidity. Guards stand on each side of the entryway from the stairwell. She says, "This floor is where we keep the lab and research subjects. That is to say, the research area is two stories but the entrance is on this level." She opens her arms, indicating the doors lining each side of the hall. "These are residential chambers." She points at a larger door just past the residential ones. "That is the gymnasium. There is a library a little further down. Beyond the library is the test subjects' communal area."

How did these people get here? Did they volunteer? I have a gut feeling that they ended up here the same way I did. Against their will.

"Is something wrong, Dr. Taylor?" Prefect Gray asks. She must have noticed my uneasiness.

"Yes," I continue. "I realize that you want me to believe we are part of the same team. The truth is, I wonder if you believe it. We both know I am a prisoner here as much as these test subjects. We never had a choice about coming here. Now that we've seen what goes on here, you can't let us leave. How do I know you will let us go once you have what you want from me?"

"Don't be so paranoid," she responds. "Once your work is done of course you will be allowed to leave. The only reason we pushed so hard to get you here is because your participation in our research is absolutely necessary for our future endeavors."

She moves to the library and opens it. Scientists traverse the spacious area, reading books in different formats: digital, halo-projected, and traditional. We continue through the hallway, which I am beginning to realize is set up like a nine square by nine square grid, based on when we reach walls and corners.

Next we come to the lab. Entering it, I see a leather medical chair which sits in the middle of the room surrounded by a glass case. The glass extends from floor to ceiling. Bands of light illuminate the room in warm hues of yellow, orange, and red, built into the floor and walls.

To the right is a protective glass case, various pieces of jewelry and some stained glass mounted on the wall behind it. Overhead is more solid white panels. To the left is a wall full of instruments. Some I am familiar with: stethoscopes, syringes, blood pressure machines, and oxygen readers.

"This is where we perform the majority of the experiments," Prefect Gray starts. "The accessories on the wall are part of the experiments. They are called Ais."

"Ais?" I ask.

"They are much easier to understand when you see how they are made," she states, turning one of the lab's empty walls into a screen. It is fascinating how the wall seamlessly melds into a visible display of lights and color.

The image on the wall is one of a medical ward. It is a circular shape with two levels and high walls, extending up well beyond any of the rooms. I see six people being kept there, and I recognize them by their files. Strangely, they appear healthier and stronger than they do in the pictures from their files; it is a stark contrast to the expectations of living in such conditions. I watch a small robot, identical to AP-11, move about the area. A thermometer on the screen indicates the temperature of the test subjects' living area is significantly higher than the rest of the facility, inhumanely hot.

"Is that temperature, correct?" I ask Prefect Gray, hoping it is some malfunction giving the high reading — 134 degrees Fahrenheit.

"It is," she confirms.

"That can't be right!" I exclaim. "How can they survive? Why aren't they all exhibiting symptoms of heat..." I stop, as I answer my own question. This is my pico-technology in humans.

"Isn't it incredible?" She notices my expression of understanding. "I assure you that the subject's enhanced bodies do not even recognize a difference in the temperature. They are much more apt to support the heat. Mythe averages about 30 degrees warmer than Earth as it circles two nearby stars. We are prepping them to help establish a new colony on Mythe. Assuming they survive, of course."

"What do you mean? People have died?"

"In a way," she explains. "But I'm not so sure 'died' is the correct word for it. I would go with 'transcended.'"

"Transcended?" I ask.

"What we have learned through our research is that not all mortal minds are capable of containing the energy generated by pico-technology. The majority of our test subjects have unfortunately been driven to the brink of insanity." She looks at me eye to eye. "For their own good and for ours, we have developed a method to transport their minds into physical objects, the jewelry and stained glass you see on the wall."

My initial reaction is of shock, but something tells me – if she realizes I'm not on her side – she may help me to 'transcend.' It is best to bide my time, learning more about what she's doing and waiting for an opportunity to help those who are still alive. I put my hands behind my back and tap a message to Syd and Alex, using my index finger against the top of my other hand. "We have to figure out how to escape and help these people being held prisoner." Aloud, I ask her, "Those objects on the wall are living people?"

Her lips curl up into a smile. "They are. Please, follow me."

We return to the hall and continue through its corridors. Still struggling to maintain composure and hiding my disgust for Prefect Gray and what she's been doing here, I remain silent. We come to a room and its door slides open. "This will be your habitation. Please, take as much time as you need here. I know you have seen a lot of new things today and have a lot to take in."

"Thank you, Prefect," I say, giving her a respectful nod of the head and reminding myself of how important appearances are going to be if I'm going to be able to understand this place. What is most important is to be able to use that knowledge to help the apparent prisoners who she calls 'test subjects.'

"You're very welcome." She turns and walks back toward the lab.

I gaze at the open doorway to my room and step inside, finding it has already been decorated, an almost perfect replica of my home; a portion of my home, anyway. It is off-putting that they were able to replicate so many intricate details of my private residence. Stepping inside with my guards, the door closes. They place their new white uniforms against the wall.

In front of us a screen flashes on, taking up the whole wall. It is the ward.

I watch as two guards enter into view and march over to a room — it is Olivia inside. They grab her by each arm and drag her out of the area. She hangs there like a rag doll but I can see that she is very much awake, scanning her eyes back and forth and allowing herself to be pulled along and toward the door leading to the hall.

"Olivia!" Amy begins to yell. "Snap out of it. Don't let them take you. Can you hear me? Please, don't let them take you!"

My heart feels for them both.

The camera shifts to the hallway, showing as the guards exit the ward and the door shuts behind them, cutting off Amy's pleas to her friend. The angle of the image continues to shift as the guard and Olivia travel down the hall and into the lab where the guards open the glass chamber, place Olivia in it, and then close the door, sealing her within. Metal bands protrude from her seat, trapping her wrists, waist, and ankles and holding her in place. Spirit broken, she offers no resistance.

A mechanical arm pinches a gold necklace next to the chamber, connected by a cable leading to Olivia's chair. That is when it clicks: they are about to turn her into an Ai. I don't want to watch but I can't turn away. Is there anything I can do to help Olivia? Is Prefect Gray telling the truth about Olivia's mind and body being too weak to contain her modified, pico-tech form? If they didn't turn her into an

Ai, now, what would happen? The questions continue to race through my mind.

"What's going on?" Syd asks treading over to me, while Alex remains unmoving. I can't bring myself to answer, nor to pull away from the screen. All I can do is watch as the scientists leave the lab. As soon as they are out they close the door and a cerulean light begins to emanate from the ground, rising from the floor to fill the room and creating a shadow outline of Olivia.

Her body begins to jerk as flashes of energy fill the chamber, like little bolts of lightning. Though I cannot hear what is going on inside the lab, it is obvious that she's in pain, now struggling to escape her restraints. Her mouth is open. I imagine the sounds of her screams being securely contained in the soundproof lab so none can hear but her.

I hear a gasp escape Alex.

Olivia's body falls limp and unmoving. The lights continue flashing for another thirty seconds or so. When they return to normalcy the scientists file back in, disconnecting the mechanical arm and taking the ring from the chamber. Looking at Olivia, her body has already begun to turn gray and her lips purple. As the scientists place the ring on the wall with the other Ais, two guards enter and remove the lifeless girl from the chamber, dragging her out of the room.

Rage burning inside me, I speak softly to Alex and Syd. "I knew Prefect Gray lacked ethics when she applied this technology to the study of humans but I never imagined this is what we'd find here."

Syd whispers, "The police will have a difficult time breaking through duranium doors, and, even if they could, the weapons they use here are well beyond what the police or military would be using. The way I see it is we need to keep playing along, bide our time, and make these people think we are on their side. There is really no other way around it. We wait for an opening."

Alex pats my shoulder, his way of saying, "Things will be tough but we can do this".

Just then, Prefect Gray's image replaces that of Olivia on my screen.

She exclaims, "You just witnessed years of research before your very eyes. Having seen it many times before, I can say with surety that this is the beginning to discovering our own immortality."

Knowing this is the moment to sell that I am on her side, I tell her, "How long did it take you to get to this point and how do you know their spirits live on in the objects?"

She answers, "There will be time for you to learn about that later".

Before I can respond, an audible explosion and ensuing shockwave rocks the entire facility and knocks me off my feet. The lights flicker until they die.

When the emergency lights turn back on, I see Syd and Alex seem to have kept their balance. Syd helps me to my feet.

"Status report," Prefect Gray's image on the screen orders. "What was the cause of that explosion?"

The image changes to the Life Bridge and I hear a man's voice begin to explain. It's a news channel. "Less than a minute ago, the rebels launched a terrorist attack on the Life Bridge, utilizing a nanotech weapon. Let's replay the footage. What you are about to see may be disturbing." A visible shockwave stems from the point of an explosion, expanding to fill the screen. The Life Bridge is a quarter of the planet away but we still felt the explosion. The video shows as the Life Bridge slowly begins to dissolve in a wave of blinking lights which expand to cover the bridge, slowly eating away at it and creating holes. The man's voice continues. "Nanobots are currently scouring the bridge and emergency personnel are on site."

The Life Bridge was designed to withstand a nuclear explosion but appears hopeless before the nanotech-driven weapon. Still, the Life Bridge had other mechanisms built in to prevent New World II from having a full-speed collision with our planet. "What about the contingency safety repulser coil?" I wonder aloud.

The door to my room slides open and Prefect Gray and AP-11 enter. "Initial reports from the terrorist rebels claim they control the safety repulser coil and that it has been disabled. The Earth's gravitational pull will bring New World II into a collision course with..." There is a pause in AP-11's voice before she continues with a stutter, "There is no way around it. Earth as we know it will be destroyed."

I can't believe it. "What?! Why would they do this? I mean, it's suicide!" The question is rhetorical but it still solicits an answer.

Prefect Gray explains. "Because, like us, they have a way off this Earth." My mind is racing.

"How much time do we have?" she asks AP-11.

"My calculations give us around twenty minutes," AP-11 answers.

She instructs. "Sedate the test subjects and initiate pre-flight procedures. Inform me when preparations have been made." The communication cuts out and she turns her attention to my guards and me. "I suggest you all take a seat. Things are about to get very bumpy." She exits the room.

A robotic voice begins speaking over the loudspeaker. "Take-off procedures initiated...take-off procedures initiated...take-off procedures initiated..." This complex is a spaceship? That can't be.

It's been said that fear is the prospect of death but calm is the certainty of it. I'd say the truth lies somewhere in the middle.

Syd is like me, a young man who never started a family. Observing him, I realize he is as worried for Alex as I am, casting sympathetic glances over at his fellow guardsman.

Alex is shaking, a blank glaze over his eyes, twitching thumbs, and a subtle rocking back and forth. "I have to get to my family." He steps toward the door but Syd grabs him by the shoulder and stops him. "Let me go." He pulls away.

"You can't get to them in time," Syd insists.

"He's right," I add. "There isn't anything you can do. Even if you could escape this facility, you'd die before you could even contact them. I'm sorry, Alex."

"I have to try!" he begs, turning to the closed door. He tries to pry it open but to no avail. Even if I wanted to help him, I wouldn't be able to open the door. Syd and I are left to watch him.

He pounds, claws, and cries until his knuckles become bloody. Refusing to give up, he puts on the white glove of his uniform, hoping it will give him leeway in opening the door. Shouting through the tears and pain, he falls to his knees — helpless and emotionally broken.

The voice of AP-11 sounds over the loudspeaker. "Subjects are sedated and secure in their rooms. They will sleep through take off and for most of the three-day journey to Mythe. We are ready for liftoff."

"No!" Alex screams.

"Alex, I'm sorry," I say, attempting to comfort him and at the same time understand Prefect Gray's words. My mind can barely comprehend what is transpiring.

"Please take your seats and fasten your restraints. Lift-off in sixty seconds," the voice commands.

A series of panels extrude from the wall next to harnesses. Syd and I lift Alex up off the floor and fasten him into his seat. We take our places on either side of him.

I close my eyes and focus, controlling my breathing and trying not to let my adrenaline get the best of me. The room is completely silent. Then there is a distant hum and soft vibration. It grows to a growl and rumble, finishing in a roaring quake. The force of gravity holds me in my seat and makes me feel nauseous as the building tears away from the Earth. This is how astronauts must have felt before gravity diffusers made their trip to space more bearable.

Things get worse as we hit the atmosphere. It is like the turbulence and loudness of an antique 747, only ten times worse.

When I feel like I can't physically and mentally withstand any more, a quiet and calm begins to replace the chaos. The shaking stops. I undo my restraints and begin to walk to a small window. My legs are like Jello, not knowing what I am about to witness.

From space, I watch as the Earth shrinks. Green and beige landmasses and white clouds begin to mesh with the color of the oceans until the planet becomes a single color, a pale blue. A simple circle against a black, starry backdrop, the resonance of sunlight glinting off its surface perhaps for the last time.

It isn't the Earth's visual value which is impressive, however: rather, its historical one. Each person who has ever been — every love story, success, failure, heartache, and jubilation — is represented there, and from my window it is no bigger than my thumbnail.

I stand there, my breath fogging the window as it escapes me in slow rhythmic beats. Alex steps next to me, tears streaming down his face as we watch the beginning of the end.

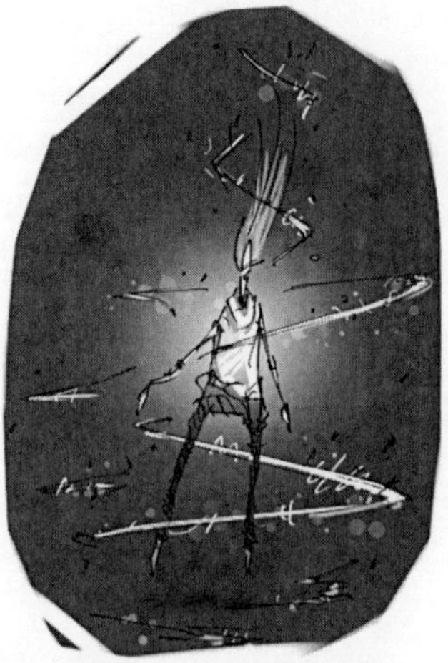

CHAPTER THREE
CRUEL INTENTIONS

The image on the wall behind us is magnified. It shows the man-made planets colliding with the natural one: crunching and igniting a brilliant white glow. When the white fades there is a brilliant red. It expands, burning up all the oxygen in the atmosphere. The intense burning red grows until it envelopes the planets. A chemical reaction within the center of one of the hulks creates a secondary explosion: shooting a ring of debris and energy out as all material within the strengthened flames disintegrates and melts together into charred bits of earth and iron. I imagine thousands of unheard voices screaming out, their sound lost in the empty void of space. The unrecognizable mass now glows a brilliant red and white as seas of magma incase them, a burning ball of matter orbiting the sun. A world whose entire history and population was lost in an instant, with the exception of us. We are all alone.

Prefect Gray re-enters the room speaking to AP-11, "Proceed to the wormhole. Keep the test subjects sedated until we have passed through and are on the Mythe side. We don't want to give the subjects any idea of what has happened."

"Yes, ma'am." AP-11 rolls out of the room. The screen turns off.

She focuses on me. "It seems that we have no choice but to work with each other."

What is wrong with you? How can you continue with the experiments after what just happened? Don't you realize what just happened? I mask these inner thoughts, asking, "What is this wormhole you keep talking about?"

"About ten years ago, with the help of our AI, we were able to figure out how to manifest wormholes: rips in spacetime that allow you to travel great distances almost instantly. We placed such a wormhole behind the moon and were able to keep it open with negative energy."

I ask, "And where will that take us? To Mythe? That is where you said we are going, correct?"

"Correct." She pauses. "It is part of a solar system in the constellation Lyra. Just over 25 lightyears away.

"About fifteen years back, we identified this unique planet. It was habitable and nearer than any other similar planet we had ever discovered. Through the use of perpetual acceleration we were able to reach the planet within an incredible four years. Now, with the wormhole in place, we can reach the planet much faster. Once we have traversed the wormhole, we will wake the test subjects and it will be just a day or two until we land."

She stretches her arms over her head, saying, "From there we should be able to sustain ourselves indefinitely. We established a rudimentary base there a few months ago. There is a rare and unique stone called mercurial that we've been mining. Its properties are fascinating — unlike anything we have ever seen before. It is an ore which has been critical in our experiments. We are the only ones on Earth..." she stops herself and rephrases before she continues. "We were the only ones to ever know of its existence. It has allowed us to do all the things which you have seen today, creating plasma weapons and Ais. As I mentioned earlier, the lifeforms on Mythe have proven to be a challenge for us."

"But then why experiment on people? Your weapons must surely be powerful enough for your defenses?" I ask.

"You would think so, but you will soon see how dangerous these creatures really are. Stone golems, sand worms, sand sharks, valkyries..." She pauses for breath. "Not only did we find life, but we found lots of it. In terms of intelligent civilizations, we have come across ruins that indicate an intelligent species was there at one time. But we have not encountered any lifeforms with intelligence that match or exceed our own."

I interject. "That didn't answer my question. Why do you need to experiment on people?"

"Because," her voice sounds like a whisper, "these people will become our most powerful weapons, the only weapons capable of allowing us to withstand every possible challenge Mythe can present." She sighs. "That is enough questions for today. In your closet you will find a wrist band to operate all the doors in the facility, as well as a lab coat identical to the one which you preferred on Earth. Between now and the time the subjects awake, I invite you to view and review their files until you've memorized them. We will update your tablet with new information in regards to Mythe, Mercurial, and Ais." She smiles. "Once you are an expert you can help us theorize about how to expand the mental capacities of our test subjects so that we no longer have to convert them to Ais."

"I'll do what I can to help." At least until I can help the prisoners escape.

She excuses herself from my room and exits, the door sliding shut behind her.

I glance over at Alex, pat him on the shoulder, and try to think of something to say. Nothing comes to mind. He squeezes his eyes together and a single tear streams down his face as he swallows, fighting to maintain his sanity.

"I am so sorry." Syd goes to sit on the other side of Alex. "Everything that has happened here is so wrong."

Thinking about the events of the day, I pat Alex's shoulder one more time, stand, and move to the window. I admire Alex's strength and courage through this. I am lucky to have my most trusted friends with me, whereas Alex does not. I continue to the window and see the wormhole as it draws nearer, like a bubble floating there in the vast darkness. We enter its perimeter, stars elongate and we flash into the emptiness of space.

We exit the other side of the wormhole in an instant, teleported to the far reaches of a foreign solar system. AP-11 is assigned to be my personal assistant and she travels everywhere with me. It makes it difficult to communicate with Syd and Alex. We continue to use Morse code and hope the robot doesn't notice. She seems to be more focused on her crocheting, in any case.

Alex spends the first day in isolation, dealing with the hurt of loss. Syd does his best to comfort his friend. I realize Syd and I may be on our own when it comes to freeing the others. Our plan involves three steps. First, we need unrestricted access to the facility. Second, we need a way to disable security. Third, we need weapons. Once we land, we will break away from this group and start a new life together. It's hard to believe that any of this is happening — or happened.

In my room I dismantle my facility armband, figuring out how it works. During reassembly I add a few new features. After we are out of here I will have to remember to thank Prefect Gray for replicating every aspect of my house. If she hadn't, I may not have been able to scrounge together each component I would need for my armband's modifications. I send AP-11 on random errands to keep her occupied.

Our second day is one of mental convalescence. Alex has passed into a stage of depression. I suspect he will remain there for some time. Still, he seems like he may be able to keep things together enough to help us with the escape plan.

Going to sleep on the second night, I feel unprepared for the morning because tomorrow is the day we wake the test subjects.

Early in the morning I am reviewing Amy's file one last time before meeting her and the others. Knowing I will be meeting them soon, I wonder what I will tell them. Do they need to know Earth has been destroyed? They probably don't, not yet. They've been through enough as it is. How can I even help them, now? We're all going to be stuck on an unfamiliar world and at the mercy of a delusional woman.

Amy's file shows her family: brothers, sisters, and parents. She even had a pet dog. How can I look her or any of the others in the eyes, knowing everything they care about and hope for is gone? I feel remorse for them.

I hear a knock on the door and say, "Come in". Syd comes through my door, wearing his white armor and holding his helmet in his hand.

Alex and Syd have been given rooms adjacent to mine, one on each side. I ask, "How is Alex?"

"Still hasn't left his room. Give him time. Alex knows we have important work to do and he won't let us down. You'll see." He sounds hopeful.

AP-11 slides through the open door and comes in, halting next to me and staring.

I ask her, "Did you need something?"

"I do," she confirms. "This morning you are going to meet all the subjects and give them individual testing."

"I'm aware."

She chirps, "I wanted to give you some details of our final phase, things we hope to implement during your tests. Are you familiar with the theory that there are four primary human emotions?"

"Yes," I nod. "That has been the prominent theory in psychology for a quarter century. Every other emotion is just a subcategory which falls under one of those."

"You are to implement these emotions into the next phase of experiments. We have five test subjects left. You are to use Habbicus as a control subject. Since he demonstrates sociopathic tendencies, he'll not be susceptible to emotional manipulation," she explains. "Before leaving Earth we managed to learn about Doug and some of his fears. We plan to use those on him in this phase of testing."

"Why are you manipulating their emotions?" I ask.

"We have noticed that certain emotions influence the growth and strength of their powers, as well as if they are to become Ais. We have already completed a smaller version of this test with others with very interesting results." She continues, elaborating, "Gable will be tested through sadness. We have a photo of his late daughter and a suit like the ones he used to wear when she was still alive."

"We will be working on keeping Amy happy by any means necessary, making her feel loved." She cocks her head. "That leaves Zuri," she explains. "She will be tested with anger."

"I see," I say to AP-11. "Why stimulate the negative emotions? If it is brain limitations causing these people to break down, why cause them more harm? Wouldn't it be better to test positive ones first and then move on to negative but only if we don't get the type of reaction we are hoping for? Gable can handle getting a picture of his daughter," I say, knowing that he may be happy to have a picture from back home, especially of someone who he loved. "Fear and anger may be very dangerous, though."

"You have sound reasoning." She widens her eyes. "You will be in charge of these experiments. Manage them as you see fit. Prefect Gray only has one request."

"Which is?" I ask.

"She wants to perform the test on Zuri herself."

I reply, "If that's what she wants, then that's what she'll get."

Thirty minutes later I enter the ward. The test subjects seem like they have fully recovered from their sedation. Seeing them face to face for the first time, I can't help but feel anxious. According to the files, previous test subjects have demonstrated a capacity for telepathy and manipulation of energy within their own bodies, using it to create sparks, ice, and fire.

Considering the Ais and how they are tied to the test subjects, I designed a light battle armor and hid Ais within it. I suggested to Prefect Gray that she do the same for Zuri's testing but she seems to have other plans.

Habbicus volunteers to come with me first. I walk him to the library, disable the cameras, let him change clothes, and return a few moments later.

Lifting his hands, he crosses them on the table, an arrogant twinkle in his eye. "Let's just cut to the chase. I can sense the energy emanating from this uniform I'm in. Why I'm here has something to do with that, right?"

"It does," I concede. "How astute of you."

"Can we move on?" he asks.

I tell him, "It is obvious you know something is different about it. I was wondering if you could tell me what is different."

He winks and smiles. "The Ais," he says. "You put Ais in it."

"You know about the Ais?" I ask.

"I do," he replies. "So, you haven't given up on turning us into weapons?"

Understanding that Prefect Gray may be watching, I reply, "We also want to help you and the others."

"There is no need to explain," he sneers. "I'm okay with becoming a weapon."

I move to the door and it opens. I say to him, "Follow me this way".

He follows me through the hallway and to a gym. I give him a glove with an Ai that is well suited for offense imbedded in its ring finger. He puts it on. Holograms start to appear and he begins to zap them with a plethora of spells, each a unique shape and color. His ability to identify targets is on borderline precognition. Before the targets even take shape, spells sail through the air, hitting their mark. As the final target disintegrates, he looks at me and asks. "What's next?"

Amazed, I watch and try to understand the science behind what just happened. How was he able to administer such control over his spells and identify the targets so freely? What I had hypothesized would happen is that he would sense some connection to the Ais in his suit but nothing beyond that.

"I hope the next test will be more challenging." His voice pulls me back from my curiosity. "You'll be asking the others the same question. Right? If they know about the suit? Let me save you some time. They'll all feel something different with it. They'll all be able to sense the Ai but it will drain most of them, sucking every ounce of energy they possess."

Ignoring his assertion, I say, "Thank you". I tap my wrist band, opening the door. "That is all I needed for today. Change your clothes and we will make our way back."

He quickly changes and then we escort him back to the living quarters.

Habbicus goes in, making his way to his room, and I invite Doug to come next. Doug follows us out of the living area. Once in the privacy of the hallway we begin to walk toward the library and he asks, "How did Prefect Gray rope you into this?"

"What do you mean?" He seems so calm, like he isn't intimidated by me in the least. Does he know something about the tests that I don't? Based on the implication of his question I can't help but wonder about the people who have worked with the test subjects before. Were they all as unwilling as I was? What happened to them in the end?

"You know what I mean," he replies.

"She recruited me because I developed a large portion of the technology she has been using." I choose to use the word 'recruited' in place of 'manipulated'.

"Pico-technology?" Doug asks.

"How did you know that?"

He answers, "I recognized you before I even heard your name, Dr. Avi Taylor. The thesis I was working on in college was about the evolution of nanotechnology. Obviously, I cited a lot of your own research and technology." He examines me, measuring my reaction.

"I'd like to think I learned some things about you as a person, too. This place doesn't seem like the type of place where you would be, not based on your moral position about the application of what you do."

You aren't wrong, I think to myself and ask, "What would you say that moral position is?"

He replies, "You know what you've created is dangerous and have worked to limit its uses and ensure it isn't used immorally. If you are here it means one of two things. Either you just learned that Prefect Gray is using it or you've had a massive change of heart in terms of your world view."

"Have you told the others about me?" I ask, opening the door to the library.

"No, it is better for them to not know about this place. The more I learn, the more I realize just how terrifying it is. I know about Ais and Apollyon." Apollyon, I remember one of the files Prefect Gray gave me being titled 'Apollyon.' I'll have to read it later. "Now it is starting to make sense. My mind has never been so clear and my body has never been so strong. That is all due to your invention, pico-technology. Isn't it? We have tiny little robots in our blood, making us stronger and smarter."

I nod, confirming his suspicion. Then I open up a cubby in the library, pull out Doug's combat uniform, and hand it to him. "This is for your test today. I'll be back in a few minutes to perform a quick test."

He forces a smile and I leave the room, hearing the door slide shut behind me. Both Doug and Habbicus seem to have a great understanding of what is going on here. Why do they comply with it all, especially Doug, who seems to understand about Ais? Has he resigned himself to some horrible fate? Is he that hopeless? Maybe he's just biding his time.

When placed in hopeless circumstances many people have been driven mad, unable to escape their emotion-driven despair. Something tells me that won't be Doug's fate. His will be something much worse. Does he understand this and is simply surviving to bide his time for his friends?

"What's wrong, boss?" Syd asks. "You look worried."

I shake my head and begin to tap a message on my leg to Syd while we wait for Doug to finish dressing. I explain that he is to write a note to Doug regarding our plan. Deliver the note to him so that he knows someone is on his side. He will be allowed to share the information at his discretion with the other test subjects. Syd nods in acknowledgement.

I turn to Alex. "How are you holding up?"

"Horribly," he answers, no emotion in his voice. "...but we have a job to do and if we don't get it done no one else will."

I pat his shoulder and the hallway enters into a comfortable, albeit remorseful silence. It is peaceful and dreadful all at once. My mind wanders into realms of possible futures, the most terrible outcomes at the forefront of my mind, pulling at every string of uncertainty, and allowing doubt to grow within me. Could we truly save Amy, Doug, Habbicus, Gable, and Zuri? A premonition whispers, "There will be casualties". Our success will not be measured in our goals but rather in our ability to escape whatever plans Prefect Gray has for all our futures. She has no intention to let me live, nor to set any of the prisoners free. The only question is when she plans to strike out. A nagging sensation makes me think it will be sooner rather than later. Still, like Doug, I will bide my time, making myself too valuable for her to get rid of right away, and I will hope for liberation.

"That should be long enough," I say, opening the door and returning to the library. Doug has changed and is sitting at the table. I sit across from him. "How do you feel in that uniform?" I question.

He closes his eyes, concentrating without saying a word. As if performing some intense physical labor, he begins to breathe more heavily, sweat forming on his brow and veins popping out in his neck. The beads on his forehead stream down his face. Some of the Ais imbedded in the fabric begin to glow. "It is connected to me," he pants, taking a pause to catch his breath.

"Are you alright?" I ask him.

"I'll be fine," he responds. "Just a little drained. It feels like I ran a marathon or something." I make a mental note of the contrast between Habbicus and Doug in terms of their reaction to the test. Why did it not faze Habbicus? Was he just further along with his development? It might be his younger age which allows him more energy. Maybe it is something else. For now I must confine myself to the simple knowledge that their reactions are different.

"Do you need anything?" I ask.

"No," he insists. "Just some rest. Are we done?"

"We are," I confirm, recognizing he isn't ready for the combat phase of testing. I leave the library, giving him a few moments to change, and then we begin the trip back. Doug walks with his hands on his hips, his body recovering from the strain of the experiment. By the time we reach the ward he shows no physical sign of his exhausted state but I note that he returns to his living area. I deduce it is to rest and recover.

Looking at the remaining people, I declare, "Gable, you are next". I am curious to meet the man known as Gable Silt, the great mind behind one of the world's greatest former technology companies. If Habbicus and Doug both understood that pico-technology was the driving force behind their experiments, then surely someone like Gable would recognize it too.

"Coming, dear," he replies, chuckles, and marches out the door.

My two guards and I follow him. Our feet echo as we pad down the empty hall. Gable moves with something which is a combination of a skip and a gallop. The strange childlike gusto for life seems inappropriate for such a dreary place. Realizing the sentiment is being exuded from one of the most brilliant minds of our time makes it that much more unsettling.

Remembering my college psych classes, I can't help but wonder if Gable's eccentric behavior is some type of defense mechanism he uses to cope with his captivity. Files indicate he is the subject who has progressed least and been here longest. It seems inconsistent with someone who has always finished at the top of his class.

As with the others, we come to the library and I let Gable change into the combat uniform before proceeding with the experiment. The Ais begin to glow almost immediately and he begins to sweat. Hoping to keep him from becoming too drained, I explain, "The suit was a test but I'm afraid you aren't ready for it yet. Try this on instead." I open another cubby and leave the room.

When I return to the room, he is in the light, brown dress suit and holding a picture in his hand. I sit across from him and observe, "You were close with your daughter?"

"Yes." His solemn tone depicts the opposite image of what he displayed in the hall. "Phoenix and I were very close. We did everything together." His eyes stray from the picture and up to me. "Thank you."

"For what?" I ask.

"This photograph." He smiles. "I know Prefect Gray meant it as a cruelty but you did so as a kindness, thinking I would benefit from it.

You were both right. It is bittersweet to see my dear Phoenix again but the benefit far outweighs the harm. Thank you."

"You're welcome," I say.

Gable speaks. "I know I didn't do as well with your testing as you would have liked. But I promise, when we get out of here, and we will, I will be more useful. Can I return to my room, now?"

I nod, trying to keep my composure. Did a memo go out explaining that Syd, Alex, and I are planning an escape? I remember the note which Syd slipped to Doug. Had Doug somehow already communicated our intent? Maybe Gable is just super perceptive. For now, I ignore his assertion. We begin the trip back, and Gable enters the ward. As he rejoins his cellmates, I say, "Amy, you are next". Looking at her, I wait.

"On my way," she says and follows me out the door, my guards taking their place behind her.

I examine her as we stride down the hall. Interacting with her, I begin to understand she has a quality which makes her different than the others. She thinks with her heart, letting her feelings dictate her actions and thoughts. Her empathetic manner of being is surprisingly accurate and effective in terms of our testing. She is able to telepathically connect with the Ais, combating the holograms with extreme efficacy, and afterward she is less drained than the others. It indicates to me that magic is based in emotion and is not so much an intellectual concept. I escort Amy to the ward and then I return to the lab.

From a screen I watch the library where Prefect Gray will be performing her test on Zuri. It doesn't take long for them to reach the room. Prefect Gray enters first, sitting at the table and signaling for Zuri to do the same. Two guards wait at the entrance.

"AP-11, turn the audio on," I say, I can hear their conversation.

Prefect Gray says, "Tell me again why you agreed to come here".

"Agreed?! You were going to kill my husband! You promised to keep him safe!" Zuri shouts. "He would have been dead right there on our wedding day if I didn't go. I came here so that he could live. You are a disgusting piece of filth."

Wrinkling her forehead, Prefect Gray says, "Someday you will understand. You are not a prisoner but an honored guest. When you realize your true potential you will be thanking me. I assure you."

Zuri deflects, "What's the point of this fucking conversation?"

"Well, let's get to that," Prefect Gray assures with a smirk. The lights in the library dim, and a hologram appears on the table. I can see Zuri in her wedding dress holding hands with her new husband. The two are smiling at each other, making their way down the aisle, people tossing flowers as the happy couple proceeds out of the chapel. Unknown to the holographic figures, four guards stand waiting just outside the church. The doors close abruptly behind them and the unseen guards tear the couple apart. I can see more guards begin to surround the church. Zuri succumbs to her capturers and is taken away. The hologram pauses.

"So brave of you. Where do you think your husband is now?" Zuri's attention is instantly drawn away from the hologram to Prefect Gray's face. Her eyes begin to well up with angry tears.

"Where's my husband?" Zuri demands.

Her face is turning red, shoulders rising and lowering in quick, panting spurts. Prefect Gray begins to laugh and the hologram resumes.

Some guards surrounding the church begin to toss what look like gas canisters through the stained glass windows, while others begin securing the exits with chains. With no way for the wedding guests to escape, the church bursts into flames. Lit by the light of the fire, the guards move towards Zuri's husband, who is being restrained nearby. A guard slowly walks towards him, lifts his gun, and two quick pulses of light hit him squarely in the chest. His body goes limp and two guards toss it into the flames. The guard that dealt the fatal blow stares at the burning building and begins to laugh. The hologram flickers off.

"I know that laugh," Zuri stutters. Her eyes are piercing. "You killed him along with both our families."

"Wrong. I've killed them all. Everyone's families," she says with an unsettling gratification.

Shock overtakes me. I cannot believe what I just witnessed. Prefect Gray is a monster.

Zuri collapses to the floor.

"Put the wedding dress on her," Prefect Gray commands as she returns to her feet and looks directly into the camera. "Let it be a reminder to never forget who really is in power here."

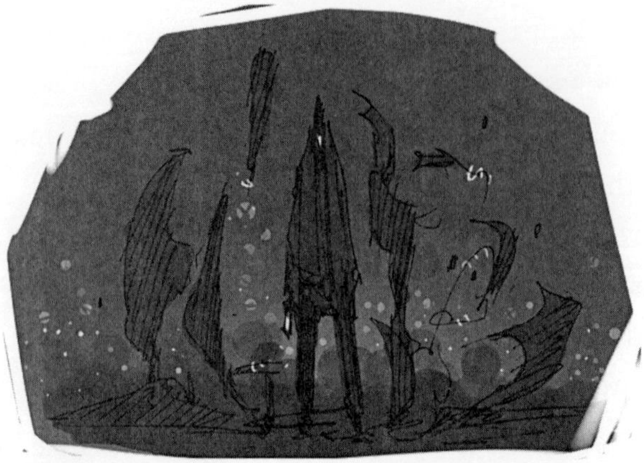

CHAPTER FOUR
KEEPING SECRETS

Zuri's unmoving body is taken to a room and left there. Her friends try to talk to her and help, but in the end, they know it is hopeless. From my room I listen to Doug's words for his comatose companion. Even AP-12 seems worried about Zuri. The small robot remains near her room, checking on her from time to time.

"You have us," Doug assures her. "You will always have us. Please, come back."

Then there is silence. I switch on the camera and watch. Zuri is lying in her bed, eyes open and looking up. Doug sits next to her, her hand in his. If only the others knew, as I have just realized, that we're being held here by murderers.

Syd's voice sounds behind me. "How bad is it?"

I glance back and see AP-11 crocheting in the corner, Syd standing next to her. I answer, "Bad. I feel for her. Our plan to get out of here is more important than ever."

Turning off the audio and visual equipment, I push my chair out from the desk, still in shock, and stand, turning to face him.

"Where is Alex?"

"Went to bed early," Syd answers. "I insisted he take a few moments to rest. He is still processing everything which has happened over the past few days. How are you holding up with all this? You haven't forgotten to take care of yourself, have you?"

"Of course not," I say. "Why do you ask?"

"Because back in the orphanage you used to get so caught up in your little projects that you'd forget to eat," he reminds me.

"We were kids then," I reply.

"You were seventeen and finishing up college," he smiles. "You have remembered to eat dinner, right?"

"Not yet. I'm not hungry," I confess.

"Just make sure you get something to eat before turning in for the night," he requests.

While we have the conversation about food we tap our real conversation, knowing we are probably being watched. How is the plan coming along?

Syd informs me that the device I made to disable the security guards worked. It looks like we will have to wait to get the weapons until just before the escape, to prevent anyone from seeing us.

I let him know that I plan to clone Prefect Gray's wristband tomorrow, which would give us unrestricted access to the facility.

Transitioning back to our vocal conversation, I promise, "I will eat before I go to sleep".

"Good," he answers with a wink, turning to leave the room. "Good night," he says, as he closes the door.

Before going to bed, I read the file regarding the place called Apollyon. Probably not the best idea. My eyes close and darkness and death saturate the air, polluting my nostrils. Walking through the depths of it, I wonder, is there any escape? The file on what can only be described as a psychological hell is still fresh in my thoughts, more terrifying than any bedtime story. The most horrible realization is that mankind created it.

Being trapped in such a place could drive a person to insanity, though I know that will not be my fate. Before long I will wake up and the screams of the fallen will no longer penetrate my ears, becoming nothing more than an unpleasant nightmare.

Wading through the darkness, hoping to find a glimmer of light, and listening to every minute sound, I feel as though my heart will beat out of my chest. Something squirms across the ground in front of me and causes me to jolt back. "It is just a mouse," I say and continue down the dusty path through the forest. Or is it a rocky mountain pass? I can't tell. It is all so dark.

The shouts and lamentations of the fallen are closer, now, begging for freedom. In reality it would be better to have never existed than to be trapped in such a place. Thump, thump, thump: my feet echo and I am in a dark hallway. I hear the rhythmic respirations of the beast who is lord of this domain. A growling yawn and the shrill cries of the lost draw nearer. I can no longer hear the growling, nor my own thoughts, just the calls for salvation: "Save me, don't forget us, HELP...HELP!"

"Let me out of here!" Waking, I force my eyes open and listen to the voice coming through the speaker in my room one more time. "HELP!" It is Doug. What is happening to him? I sit up in bed and he continues to beg for rescue. Realizing I am no longer dreaming, I swing my legs over the edge of my bed and hurry out the door. Not even bothering to change out of my pajamas, I make my way down the hall and to the lab.

Not to my surprise, a team of scientists is there, huddled around a screen. Pushing my way through them, I identify the image they watch as a room in the ward. One of the beds has vanished into the tiles beneath the room, encasing the occupant like a tomb. Amy comes into view, pounding and pushing against the box. "Lazarus, can you hear me?" she says. "Please, it is going to be okay. I'm here. Talk to me!"

I continue to watch and she is eventually able to free her brother through the help of AP-12. Luckily, only hours before, I had re-programmed him to ensure their safety.

"How very interesting," Prefect Gray chimes from the entrance to the lab. "Although I would have liked Doug to be imprisoned for longer. He got out far too soon. Why did that robot do that? That wasn't supposed to happen. Avi, I need you to take a look at its AI first thing tomorrow morning."

I turn to her — realizing that if I can get a little closer I can clone her wristband — and walk over. Being in her presence for the first time since the Zuri incident is unnerving. "Sure thing." Glancing down, I don't see her wristband on her wrist. How is she moving about the facility? The security systems must be programmed to just recognize her face. She had a wristband before. Did she catch on to our plan? Is there any other way we can gain access to the facility?

She grins. "We will be arriving on Mythe soon and we will need our test subjects ready once we do, understood?"

"Yes." I walk out of the room. Instead of returning to my quarters, I decide to stop by Prefect Gray's on the off-chance I may be able to find her wristband and clone it. When I arrive at her door, I pause and wait for guards to pass. Using one of my wristband's modifications, I hack her door and attempt to open it. Seconds seem much longer, each moment feeling like it could be my last. Finally, the door clicks open.

Inside, I find her wristband on a nightstand by her bed. Running a new program on my wristband, I begin to copy all the codes and specifications of hers. A scuffling sounds outside and I hear Prefect Gray's voice. Glancing at my band, I see I just need a few more seconds. Taking her wristband, I slip to the doorway and peek outside. She is distracted by one of the scientists. I see it has completed copying. Hurrying to place her wristband back in its place, I slip into the hall, closing her door behind me. Just as it shuts, she turns and walks over to me. "Avi, did you need something?"

"Yes, Prefect," I reply. "I just wanted to wish you a good night." I'm hoping she buys it.

She pauses for a second before speaking. "Interesting. It is late. If you'll excuse me." She slips into her room. "Good evening."

"Good evening," I repeat.

I don't sleep much the rest of the night. There was no way I could.

The next morning I am guided by guards to the helm of our spaceship, which happens to be on the top floor. Prefect Gray is next to me, speaking in a long-range communicator to someone I've never seen before.

Prefect Gray tells the man onscreen, "We will be arriving shortly and when we do I have something I would like to show everyone. Consider this a formal invitation to witness the final phase. Is your ship due to arrive at the same time?"

It is both shocking and alleviating to realize there are survivors from Earth beyond those in this facility. I wonder how many other 'ships' there are.

"Indeed, we are," the man replies. "You are finally willing to divulge the details of what you've been working on, Prefect?" The man seems surprised and shaken. He is probably feeling the same nervousness as me, one brought about by our mass exodus to a new planet. "I do hope it is what you have promised. With the golems, valkyries, and sand worms, it is critical that we have a defense beyond our common weapons. We won't last but mere days without some sort of defense. It has already been shown our energy weapons are useless against the worms."

She replies, "What I have been working on will restore everyone's hope at our chances of survival. It will not disappoint. I assure you. You will see what I mean when we arrive."

He politely nods and the communication cuts out.

Unable to restrain myself, I ask, "How many other facilities were there like this?"

Prefect Gray explains. "There were sixteen of our facilities that were strategically placed around the world. Our branch's purpose was to focus on the defense systems to protect our assets on Mythe. We built two docks on Mythe — each with the ability to house eight facilities." She pauses and stretches before continuing. "The docks are large circular structures and as such have been named the Life Rings. They can provide for all our natural needs for generations as we establish our presence."

Something about how she says, 'establish our presence' makes me uneasy, like she has some delusional conquest scenario planned out and ready to execute. Knowing her, she probably does, I remind myself. Trying to keep my disgust to myself, I question, "When will we arrive?"

"Tomorrow morning," she replies. "In the meantime, you will continue the tests on the subjects." She steps closer to me, so only inches separate her face from mine. As uncomfortable as the situation is, I don't flinch.

"I understand," I tell her.

"We have an interrogation room in the back of the library," she explains. "Prep that for today. In the meantime, I will be informing the others."

"As you wish," I tell her, and begin the trip to the library. On the way, I disable the guards outside the science lab, slip in, and grab an Ai. I am careful to pick an Ai which the test subjects will know, Olivia. Once I have the Ai safely tucked away, I finish my journey to the library.

I prep the room for a test. Once prepared, I turn on the microphone to the ward and hear an argument between Habbicus and the others. "Enough." I cut the debate short. "Amy, you will be first. Today's evaluation will be significantly longer than yesterday. Are you ready to go?"

"Bye," I hear her say. "I really don't feel like talking today. But since I know you aren't going to give me a choice, we may as well get it over with."

"Yes, we may as well," I repeat, ignoring the sarcasm in her tone. "The guards will bring you to your next test. They are waiting outside the door," I say, and make the door beep and open. "Get going. We have much to discuss, about last night and about the future."

"If you say so," she retorts.

I consider what I've learned about Ais and Apollyon. At first I thought an Ai to be the mere mapped-out human brain being transferred to some database within an object, an electronic copy of the person and not the actual person.

However, there was a man named Duncan MacDougall who once hypothesized about the spirit of a person having mass. His tests determined said weight to be around an ounce. In creating a new Ai there is an inexplicable weight increase within the item containing the Ai, which coincides with Dr. MacDougall's testing. Could it be the soul is transferred with the genetic and electronic data?

If that is, in fact, the case, then Apollyon has just become much worse. I recently learned that to ensure an Ai's compliance with their counterpart's orders, a mechanism has been built into each of them. If an Ai disobeys the person holding it, then its electronic form is teleported from the object and to a database within the facility's server. That database reads the mapped-out mind of the individual, searching for their own fears. In essence, it forces the Ai's soul to be living in their own personal version of a hell. To ensure the soul isn't lost, Ais are also teleported to Apollyon when the reciprocal holding them is destroyed. If I had to predict what sick mind came up with Apollyon as a form of forcing Ais to do their work, my guess would start and end with Prefect Gray.

Standing, I watch the door to the interrogation room open. Amy walks through the doorway. From the other side of reflective glass I watch her and say, "Thank you for coming."

I am about to begin the psych evaluation when she raises her eyes, staring straight at me, her vision fixed. It is a sad look and an inquisitive one, like she is asking for help and answers all at once. All I can do is stare back and watch as she stands, tilts her head, and continues to inch closer. Her eyes don't shift to the left or the right. They just stare straight ahead, at me and through me. I feel completely vulnerable.

When she is a few inches away she pauses, lifting the palms of her hands to her cheeks. Placing my own hand on the glass, I feel a renewed vigor and an unwavering purpose. I raise my palm to the glass, fingers spread, and I push against it, wishing the glass weren't there to separate me from her. I don't care if we are going to a new planet. Amy deserves a chance at a new life and so do the others.

"Are you okay?" I ask.

The question was a mistake. She explodes, shouting at me and falling to her knees. I rush in to comfort her but am only with her a few seconds when the door to the interrogation room slides open and Prefect Gray enters. "That is quite enough. I want to see you in my office, Dr. Taylor. Now. Guards, return Amy to the ward."

I watch Amy escorted out of the room and then focus my attention on Prefect Gray. By the door she stands, glaring at me. "I gave you strict orders to avoid contact with the test subjects. Your carelessness could have been detrimental to the safety of us all."

I play along. "I am sorry. She seemed harmless enough and I was worried about her wellbeing. If we are to keep her as our happy subject, we couldn't allow her to be in that negative state of being."

"It was not your call to make," Prefect Gray snaps.

Even feeling like I am remotely associated with her and her plans makes me sick to my stomach. How can people willingly work for her and live with themselves? Or does anyone willingly work for her? I wonder how much the guards and lower level staff actually know about what goes on here. The one thing I do know – Amy is about to know. Unable to keep her in the dark anymore, I'm going to tell her of my plans tonight.

Retreating to my habitation for the remainder of the day, I send Syd and Alex to their own rooms, advising them to rest up. Tomorrow will be a big day for us. With Lazarus and the final phase beginning, attention should be off of the other test subjects. It leaves me with a decision. Do I try to save the others at Lazarus's expense? Is there a way to save all of them?

AP-11 approaches me. "Sir, I need to inform you that we are about to begin the reentry procedures beginning our descent to Mythe. Please take a seat and fasten your restraints."

I feel the facility beginning to shake and I sit down. The vibrations continue and intensify. I try to ignore them, pondering the fate of Lazarus and the others and coming to the conclusion that it will be Lazarus's decision if he is willing to serve as a distraction.

We touch down, the vibrations stop, and the facility enters into a calm.

"We have successfully linked up with the Life Ring. You are now safe to undo your restraints. Welcome home, sir," the small robot chirps. Halting all movement in an instant, she raises a hand to her head and then turns to me. "Be careful, should you decide to move about the facility. I was just informed our power systems were knocked out upon entering Mythe's atmosphere. We are working to re-route power. It is the same with all of the facilities."

"I'll be careful," I promise, watching as AP-11 exits my habitation. Moving to my window, I glance outside.

From the window of my room not one, but two suns are setting. One after the other. We're here. Will our escape plan work? Do we even know where to go? There are more questions in my head than answers.

Sand extends out in lazy dunes. Their surface shifts with the breeze, glinting as specks of the ever-moving sand catch the suns. I've never seen anything comparable. It is almost like the sand is a calm ocean whose surface shifts with the current, calm and inviting. Still, instinct shouts it is anything but safe.

The guards are disabled from the power system going down. I hear the artificial heating quiet and then the lights click off, in my room and in the hallway. I wait for all movement outside to cease and then another thirty minutes more just to be safe.

Changing into a black t-shirt and jeans, slipping into the hallway, and deciding it best not to draw attention to myself, I creep toward the lab in complete darkness. With every clink of the air purifier or distant echoing clank my heart accelerates and beads of sweat form on my brow. I wipe them away. Power may be restored at any minute. A faint swoosh of air, like the sound of the wind, resonates around each corner. Is it an imagined sound or something else? As horrible as this place is it must have its ghosts, not that I believe in such things.

The same strange whistling and clatters echo: quiet, impactful, and as if to promise I will be discovered any second. When I reach the ward AP-12 seems to be unpowered in the corner. I use my wristband and run a quick diagnostic to make sure he is disabled. When I see he is, I open the door to the ward and sneak in. First I need to speak with Doug. I find him but not in his room. Instead I find him outside his cell.

"Doug, over here, quick!" "I knew you'd be coming," he says with a smile, as he makes his way towards me, "Just call me Lazarus. Everyone else does. So, this all ends tomorrow, doesn't it?"

"One way or another," I confirm.

"Look, if you can save the others and get them out of here then do it. Just promise you'll do anything you can to save my sister Amy. Only come back for me if you get a chance...that's if I even survive the final phase."

Lazarus and I lock gazes. "I promise. And if we can, we will come back for you." We shake hands. "I'm not sure what the final phase means yet. But if we can do anything, we will."

"Thank you," he whispers.

Moving to Amy's room next, I stand by her bunk and whisper. "Amy...Amy...wake up, Amy!" Opening her eyes, she sees me and they open even wider, like she is going to scream. I hold my finger to my lips, saying, "Shh...I have something to show you. I wanted to answer your questions before but Prefect Gray wouldn't allow it. If you come with me now, tonight, I can show you everything and no one will ever have to know."

"You're crazy," she whispers. "How do I know you aren't tricking me? Tomorrow, will my friends wake up and I'll be gone? Will they never know what happened? Sorry, I feel much safer right here."

I reply, "It has nothing to do with trickery. You are curious and seeking answers. I have those answers, and I'd rather Prefect Gray be mad at me than you be mad at me. We need to go now, though. The security system and cameras are rebooting after the earthquake earlier. Who knows how much longer they will be down. So are you coming? Are you ready to know what's been going on here?"

"I am." She relents.

She follows me to my habitation, where I introduce her to Artemis, who was once her friend Olivia. I explain we are on the same team and she appears to believe me.

Knowing our time is limited, we make our way back to her room, careful not to disturb anyone. She smiles at me and thanks me. As I pull away to leave, I whisper a final piece of advice. "Amy, be careful. Tomorrow everything changes."

Once out in the hall I feel that I am home free. Amy safely has the Ai and Lazarus's convictions have helped me to become strong in my own. Abandoning caution, I don't recognize the footsteps following behind me, not until they catch up with me outside of my bedroom and I turn around to see Prefect Gray. My heart drops. How long has she been following me? Did she see me leave the ward? I try to play it off. "Good evening, Prefect."

Skipping salutations, she asks me, "What are you doing out and about?"

"I couldn't sleep," I lie, hoping she hasn't caught on to my intended betrayal. "So I took a walk to burn off some energy."

"It is awfully late for a walk," she observes. "Tomorrow is a big day for everyone, so I will jump straight to the point."

Leaning closer so her face is nose to nose with mine, she glares and hisses, "It seems as if you are enjoying your new unrestricted access to this facility". She pauses. "I saw you exiting my room. Maybe you should be more careful next time. I have already been too lenient with your requests." She looks over at Syd's door and then at Alex's, making her intentions clearly understood.

We stand in each other's presence for what seems likes hours. Prefect Gray turns and walks off. I give a sigh of relief.

"Oh, and Dr. Taylor," she says, pausing and turning back to face me. "You are right. Tomorrow everything does change. Goodnight."

CHAPTER FIVE
BEGINNING OF THE END

Though I'd never consider myself religious, I can't help but close my eyes and pray for a successful escape today. Prefect Gray is on to us, but how much does she really know? Is she aware of our plan? Gazing upon the desert, I'm not entirely sure of where we'll go or how we'll survive. A ring around the planet creates a streak of bright, rainbow colors, angling across the sky at forty five degrees. There is an irony in its beauty.

The door creaks open behind me and I turn to see Alex and Syd. Each has a backpack and Syd is carrying another in his arms. They loosen the straps and pile the packs into a corner. "These supplies should be enough to keep us alive, at least until we can find an ample supply of water and..." Syd pauses as his eyes see the desert outside. "Are you sure about this? Surviving in a rainforest or grassland is one thing. Going into a desert is another. If we wander out into that we may not last long."

"And what other choice do we have?" I respond. I catch their eyes and whisper, "She's on to us. I am not sure how much of our plan she knows about, but we have to be extremely careful moving forward."

Alex and Syd both seem a bit taken back. Alex squints and steps closer to the window and sighs.

"So what is the plan exactly?" Syd asks.

I reply, "The final phase should begin soon, which promises to be an important event. As it's happening, we get the test subjects and these supplies." I point to the bags. "And we get out of here as quick as we can. Security systems are back up and I'm sure there will be guards on the lower floors, so we will need to see how many and their positions, then we will play it by ear. We may be able to jump from one of the lower floors and not have to leave out the front door, since the sand should break our fall."

Syd states, "No matter what happens, it seems we are going to have to play things by ear and adapt".

"Right," I agree.

AP-11 approaches. "Prefect Gray requires your presence in the auditorium now, sir. The final test is about to begin."

"On our way," I tell her, and we follow her down the hall, to the elevator, and into the auditorium.

The auditorium resembles a sports stadium: multiple levels reaching high, the lowest point being a field in the center. In this case the field is made of sand.

Standing next to Prefect Gray, I watch people wander about the arena: intermingling and sipping on champagne. Some of them are physically in the domed area with us while others are holograms of people attending the event from the comfort of their own facilities. The only way to tell them apart is a slight translucency and the lack of a shadow attached to the holograms.

"Prefect Gray." One of the holograms glides over to us, floating orb projecting the image. "Good to see you."

"You as well," she nods, turning to me. "Avi, this is Prefect Froth. He is head of one of the facilities at the second Life Ring. They are responsible for developing a sustainable energy source for our operations. Prefect Froth, this is our lead scientist, Avi."

"Avi Taylor?" he asks, and I nod yes. "It is very nice to meet you, Dr. Taylor. Your pico-technology has been instrumental in our studies here. Just yesterday we observed an average increase in solar energy output of nearly seven percent."

"Solar energy?" I repeat, wondering if he has any idea what Prefect Gray has been working on.

"Of course we have not been functioning as long as Prefect Gray's site. We are anxious to see some of her research up close. Up to this point we have worked independently from each other. It will give me peace of mind knowing what new weapons will be protecting us, considering all the events over the last forty-eight hours." Glancing over at Prefect Gray he says, "Today we hope to learn more about... what were they called again?"

"Ais." Prefect Gray smiles.

"Right, Ais."

He doesn't even know what Ais are? I ask myself. How much has Prefect Gray been keeping from everyone? How surprised are they going to be after today? What will their reaction be?

The crowd of holograms and people begin to quieten down. My place is next to Prefect Gray and near an exit. As if we are about to begin a movie or a play, the lights begin to dim, leaving a beam focused on the ground in the middle of the auditorium.

Prefect Gray descends the steps into the light. She gazes out into the auditorium and prepares to speak. A microphone amplifies her voice. "Thank you all for coming.

"I will not waste your time with pleasantries. We have been working hard to develop a defense system worthy of Arc Industries. We've made many advances and are now confident in the fact that we can defend our facility and even expand further out into the desert. Without further ado, I present to you our first line of defense."

The light over her dims and focuses on some guards holding weapons. Cages sit next to the guards. Each holds a large creature resembling a scorpion. I assume they are a native species of Mythe. The cage doors lift up and the creatures leap out, charging at the guards. Using the plasma-based weapons, the guards level them with little effort. The light dims and a new one forms around Prefect Gray. The auditorium erupts in applause.

She smiles. "These plasma weapons and guards are more than capable of eliminating smaller threats." Her forehead wrinkles. "But we needed something more to deal with the bigger threats on Mythe, and for that, I have something very special to show you all today. I have developed something called Ais. Please, enjoy."

A hologram fills the auditorium as a documentary type presentation goes over the creation of Ais and how she has infused magic into human test subjects. The end of the video shows Habbicus and Amy zapping holograms in the gym. I hear some banter among the crowd, some inspired by what they are seeing and others terrified by it. The presentation ends and the light returns to Prefect Gray. More applause.

She beams, proud of what she has created, and explains, "And, there is one more thing. For the first time, right in front of your very eyes, we will create a new kind of Ai, a living Ai. So powerful, and already adapted to this environment. They will become our ultimate weapon."

The lights in the whole auditorium turn on and Prefect Gray returns to her seat beside me. The sand opens up, revealing a platform, and it rises. A massive sand worm lies there, surrounded by scientists who are armed and standing by the thick cables tethering the beast down. Some audible gasps are heard. A table like the one in the Ai lab is next to the worm and connected to the creature. With a sinking feeling, I realize Lazarus's terrible fate.

A shuffling in the hall pulls my attention away from the worm and to Lazarus. Guards are escorting him into the room, one on each arm. He complies with them, walking willingly and looking around. The scientists and holograms begin to crane their necks to get a better view. Lazarus's eyes meet mine as he is passing by. We both understand what he wishes to say.

Looking at him eye to eye, I nod, hoping he understands I will fulfill his request, and the guards pull him away. Together the three complete their journey to the chair. The guards strap Lazarus down and he remains stoic and calm, bravely facing what he knows is about to come.

Glancing at my guards, I see Syd slipping out of the room, on the way to get the supplies. Alex remains a few paces behind me, against the exterior wall of the arena.

Pushing a panel on the armrest of her chair, Prefect Gray activates a microphone. "Lazarus," she says. "You remember what happens to Ais who are disobedient."

"I do," he says back to her.

"Very well then," she replies. Then directing her attention to the science team, "Begin the experiment".

One of the scientists pulls a lever and the lights go from dim to off. Sparks fly from the connection points between Lazarus and the worm and he begins to scream, his body writhing in pain.

Unable to watch, I turn away and cringe. Some of the scientists gasp upon witnessing the torture. Others are intensely focused, coming to understand what Prefect Gray has accomplished – putting a human soul inside the body of a dangerous animal.

The fluctuating light created by the sparks stops, and so do the screams, telling me it is done. Forcing myself to look, I see Lazarus's body has already begun to take on the gray hue of death. The worm twitches on the ground. Writhing, it begins to mutate, growing in size. New seta spring from its side, some with characteristics reminiscent of human hands. Tusks widen and extend. Lazarus — is it Lazarus? — howls, slamming against the walls.

Then the creature freezes. Is it dead? I wonder.

Prefect Gray uses caution. I don't think she expected such a transformation. "Lazarus," she says softly, "can you hear me?" The worm's head shifts as if listening to the words. "Do you understand?"

The worm rolls onto its belly and its head begins to rise, slow and wobbly. Its head shakes a few times then freezes, fixated on the human body it once inhabited. Seeing without eyes, it stares and appears to contemplate.

Then it shoots forward, snapping the restraints, like a mantis capturing a fly, and devours its former body in one quick gulp. The worm looks out into the auditorium and gives an ear-piercing roar.

Chaos ensues. A woman onlooker who was one of the holograms screams. Drawn to the sound, Lazarus lunges and slams down into the person as her image fades and disappears. Metal twists and seats and bodies are thrown in every direction from the force of the collision.

More screams and carnage, hologram after hologram disappears, and those who are physically present begin to stand and run. Turning to Prefect Gray I see she is already gone, and I follow her lead. As I move toward the exit I hear metal grinding, and drowned-out screams, signifying lives being lost.

I see Alex to my right moving to meet me at the exit. I arrive before him and turn to check how far away he is. He shouts, "Look out!" Glancing behind me, I see the monstrous silhouette of Lazarus preparing to strike. As he surges forward, the weight of Alex colliding with me pushes me out of the way and I fall to the ground.

"Alex!" I shout.

Alex turns as the monster lunges forward and devours him. He is gone. In disbelief, I rise to my feet and rush out the exit. Running through the halls toward the test subjects, the ground shakes and I can hear Lazarus unleash another unearthly roar. I stand with my back against a wall, catching my breath. I can hear screams coming from the hallway I just came from. Prefect Gray runs past me, being chased by one of the scorpion creatures.

I peer around the corner.

As she runs, she abruptly stops. I see something blocking her path, a white, glowing personage forming in the darkness. The blurry and menacing light inches closer and closer to Prefect Gray. She is trapped. Her eyes dart to mine.

"Help me!" she yells.

I turn away and make my way to the ward. She releases one last final scream and then she can be heard no more.

In the hall I find AP-11. She has been torn to pieces and is strewn next to a fallen guard. I retrieve the guard's plasma gun. I reach the test subjects in the ward, blowing away some debris from the door so that they can be freed. I never imagined our escape plan to play out this way.

We make our way through the facility, step by tortuous step, until we are all safely outside the crumbling edifice.

Gathering my senses, I hear a shriek and look over towards the sound. It is Amy. Lazarus is hovering above her, as she lies on her back, defenseless. Groping nearby, I find a plasma rifle and raise it, putting the creature in my crosshairs. Do I shoot the creature that is Lazarus, knowing he is the reason we were able to escape? Is it really still him? I continue to watch, and Amy — from shock or fear... maybe both — faints, her head falling back against the soft sand.

Lazarus leans back as if preparing to lurch. Knowing I must keep my promise, my finger nears the trigger. I must keep Amy safe. But he lunges not at Amy, rather, in the opposite direction. He disappears into the rolling dunes of the desert.

CHAPTER SIX
EMOTIONS & EXPLANATIONS

A warm breeze blows flecks of sand against my face as the ultraviolet rays of the suns beat through a cloudless sky, radiating a heat which I can already feel in my skin and bones. Hurrying over to Amy, I slow, kneel next to her, and place my hand below her neck. "Are you okay?" I ask gently.

Dazed, her eyes blink open and she asks, "What was that? Where are we?"

"We'll get to that," I tell her. "For now we need to get to safety. The building is still unstable and more of it could collapse or it could explode. It's not safe to stay here."

Syd is on the ground, holding his ankle. I help Amy to her feet and we move over to him. "It's broken," he declares. "I know it is."

"Let me see," Amy says, kneeling and looking at the ankle. Syd protests and starts to pull away, when she glares at him.

"Just let me at least try to fix it. You won't be much use to us with a broken ankle. We need you out here, Syd. This may hurt."

Syd grimaces, preparing to have his ankle reset. Running her hand up and down the fracture, I see a strange glow envelop her hand and extend to the wound. The bone mends in an instant.

"Whoa, thank you. That was...that was incredible," Syd says, his eyes wide as saucers.

"Wow, that actually worked," Amy says, surprised.

"What just happened?" I ask.

"I think she fixed it," he says, raising his ankle and rolling it back and forth. I help him to his feet and he tests it. "Yup, she fixed it. Won't you look at that!"

We walk to our supply packs and Ais, grab them, and move away from the Life Ring until it is a small glint in the distance. An occasional explosion is heard in the distance and smoke pollutes the sky above it. When things have stabilized and it is no longer dangerous, we will return to the wreckage and scavenge anything useful.

We make our way to a rocky outcropping and use the supply packs to set up a canopy to shelter us from the ever-increasing gusts of wind and the blistering rays of heat. Mythe's reflective ring shifts colors with the movement of the suns, a plethora of different combinations; green, pink, and blue, to teal, white, and yellow. I have never seen anything like it.

Everything is set for the night and Syd has started a fire to cook a meal. Twilight has found us, turning the azure sky pink and then black. With unfamiliar constellations overhead, it reminds me of my first night spent in a different hemisphere, only this time there is no Southern Cross and some of the stars seem closer.

Drawn to the flame, some of the other survivors of Life Ring I make their way to us, one or two at first and then they arrive by the dozens. All of them are scared, in shock, and some tending to injuries.

Amy helped us set up the camp but now she sits on its edge. Making my way over to her, I sit, and she asks, "Where is Lazarus?" I see the pain of loss and distrust in her eyes and realize I am not ready to answer her question. I've been so focused on planning the escape I haven't even begun to think about how to explain all that has happened, nor about Lazarus and her family.

"Safe," I pause, considering how to continue. "I will tell you more in the morning. Please, just try to get some rest."

"Tell me," she begs, a quiver in her voice.

"I'm sorry," I say. "I can't...I don't know how. There are so many things that happened and I'm not sure how to explain them all. I will tell you everything in the morning and answer whatever questions you have. For now you should eat something and get some sleep."

She is about to protest, when I raise my finger to my lips, eying the survivors behind me.

"Now is not the place nor time," I whisper.

I wait for her to say something else and when she doesn't I stand, pat her shoulder, and walk over to the fire.

A flash overhead catches my eye. Turning my attention upward, I see another, like a shooting star burning up in Earth's atmosphere. The occurrence repeats time and time again and I try to understand what it means.

"It is the other ships," Enkidu says.

"What do you mean?" I ask.

He explains. "We're not the only ones who tried to escape. Some of them must have known about Mythe or maybe they just followed us here. Oddly, it looks as if their ships are burning up in the atmosphere."

I don't know what to say, so I don't say anything at all, knowing that each of those streaks across the sky represents the end of humanity — dying inside their burning hulls.

There are certain moments in life when the very soul aches, the center of a person's being: when a loved one passes away, or a child suffers. Anguish pollutes emotion, seeding itself and expanding to stifle personal growth and destroy hard-earned talents. A sense of insignificance and helplessness take place of confidence and desire. That is when a person truly dies.

Watching the night sky and observing each flash of death, I realize this is the moment where humanity faces its greatest heartache. It is ironic in a sense, the beauty inherent in such an impactful moment. Still, I can only imagine the silent screams of the lamentations which will go unheard but never forgotten.

The next morning I awaken to a pink sky. Sitting up, I attempt to brush the sand out of my hair.

Syd and some of the other surviving guards take turns on watch. He must be on duty and stands vigilant nearby. Trudging through the soft sand, I come to him and ask, "What is your honest opinion? Do you think we will be able to make it out of this place?"

"All we can do is try," he says. By not giving a direct response, he answered my question, that he didn't feel we were going to make it. "By the way," he adds, pointing to the top of the cliff where I see Amy's silhouette, "she has been up there for about two hours. You should go talk to her."

"You let her go alone?" I question.

"The only way up is through those steps." He points over my shoulder. "I've been keeping an eye on her. She's safe."

I nod and leave Syd to his sentry duties. Wandering around the base of the cliff, I search for the path up. The morning breeze has wiped away any traces of her footprints, leaving me no trail to follow. Eventually I find a winding alley cut into the rock face and follow it.

A manmade stairway — is it still called 'manmade' if a different race created it? — guides me to the top of the cliff, allowing me to find Amy. Taking one more deep breath and thinking about what to say, I pace over and lower myself to the ground next to her. Her hair is blowing in the breeze.

Looking out, I can clearly see a mountain range in the distance for the first time and it takes my breath away: uniquely situated with desert on all sides and jagged, sedimentary bluffs extending hundreds of feet up. Their most unique feature is an eerie teal glow within all the rocks, possibly created by some type of gemstone. The glowing gemstones jut out of the rock faces at certain points, sending beams of glowing volumetric light into the sky and reflecting off the peaks.

She stays reserved, still trying to understand all that is going on. While I consider how to begin, it is she who eventually breaks the silence. "We're not on Earth, are we?"

"No," I reply. "We are on a planet called Mythe. About 25 lightyears away from Earth."

"How did we get here?" Her voice gives off no emotion, no indication of what she's thinking. Her face is flat and red from too much crying.

"We were in a facility disguised as a building, but in reality, a vessel able to take us here."

"What about home? How will we get back?" she asks.

My head drops, water forming in my eyes. My voice breaks as I explain. "We won't...There was...an attack...Earth was...destroyed."

Unable to continue, I feel a single, stray tear running down my cheek. I feel awful for her. How must she feel: connecting the dots, that her family and everyone she ever cared about are dead? Everything she ever knew is gone.

Her emotions overcoming her, she begins to shake and cry. Unsure of how she will react, I put my arm around her shoulder to comfort her and she leans into me. I hold her in my arms; we don't say anything. We just cry and watch the suns rise, turning the dusky, pink sky into a brilliant, clear sapphire. Wispy cirrus clouds hold place high in the sky. The impressive mountains contrast with the smooth dunes. Sitting there in silence the tears eventually pass...but we both know the sadness of loss never will.

I don't know how much time passes when she eventually asks, "Where is he?"

Unsure of how to explain, I decide it is best to just say it.

"His soul was transferred into the giant worm we saw. It was Prefect Gray's final test. To create a living Ai."

She hangs her head. "I thought so."

"Huh?" I am caught off guard.

"I didn't realize it at the time but after I fainted and woke up, I recognized him. I could feel part of him in the worm...somewhere. He was in a dark place, lost...and scared." She considers something and then asks, "Is there any way to get him back?"

"I don't think so," I tell her. "I'm sorry."

We remain in silence a few more moments, gazing upon the glowing mountains. The cirrus clouds have been replaced with dark stratus and cumulonimbus, a strange sight, considering the rolling desert. I can't imagine it rains that often. What is more unusual is the placement of the billowing masses in the sky — forming directly over the mountains. Lightning firing and thunder blaring, a storm is born over the peaks and carries with it an uneasy sentiment.

"Avi!" Syd's voice shouts behind me and I turn to look. "We have a problem. I need to talk to you." And my sense of foreboding continues to grow.

We hurry down to the bottom of the cliff. I ask, "What is it?"

Syd explains. "I'm not sure when it happened but some of the Ais are missing."

"Maybe they fell out of one of the bags," I suggest.

"Maybe," he answers.

Realizing that losing the Ais would be another terrible turn of misfortune, I tell him, "We need to send someone to search for them. At the same time, they can retrace our steps to look. Then we scavenge the remains of the facility for food and water."

He answers. "That sounds like a plan. I can lead it, then meet you back here, while you figure out the next place for us to go. We can't stay here forever."

"Perfect. If there's any good news, we packed enough supplies for a small group: you, the test subjects, me, and ..." And Alex. I finish the sentence in my head. We still haven't talked about what happened to Alex. The fact that he wasn't with me when we reunited was all Syd needed to know.

"Alex saved my life and he believed in a life after death. Maybe he's with his family right now and happy."

"Maybe he is," Syd repeats. Syd and I share a moment of silence.

"Well, we have to care for all these people we didn't account for with our original plan."

At some point Enkidu had crept close enough to overhear the conversation, and he interrupts, saying, "The mountains".

Turning to him, I ask, "What do you mean 'the mountains'?"

"Those clouds above them," he explains. "Might mean water. We may find wild game we can eat or someone who can help us if we get to the mountains. Our food and water problems will be solved there." Taking a moment for pause, he smiles and adds, "Or we will not find any of those things and all die horrible deaths in a delirious state of thirst and hunger".

An uncomfortable silence overtakes the conversation before I finally am able to agree. "We should move to water. Thirst will be the first thing to get us. If we find food there, even better. Syd, are the weapons safe?"

"They are; no doubt we may encounter creatures on the journey. I don't expect a warm welcome here," he responds.

It is interesting to see Enkidu temporarily transition back in his element as a natural born leader. The rest of the morning is spent salvaging what we can from the destroyed Life Ring. Unfortunately, no sign of the Ais was found. That afternoon we all meet to discuss the plan.

We present the idea to the rest of the group and are met with a plethora of different opinions about how we should survive. One man suggests we stay where we are, digging our own well while living off the supplies we have. Another suggests that Amy, Enkidu, and Twigs figure out how to create water through their magic. Then, of course, we have Enkidu's plan.

"I truly believe Enkidu's plan is our best option," I argue. "We don't know if their are any aquifers for a well and Twigs, Enkidu, and Amy do not have the abilities to create water out of thin air. We don't even know if there is water here — everything is a guess."

One of the scientists argues — I recognize him as the hologram I met at Lazarus's creation, the one who was the leader of one of the other facilities — I believe his name was Prefect Froth.

"And who put you in charge, Dr. Taylor? It was Prefect Gray and your facility who got us in this mess in the first place. I suggest we find a way to repair our long-range communicator and call Life Ring II for help. They can get here in a matter of days."

Twigs jumps in and surprises me with his support of Enkidu. "We can reach the mountains in a day at most. With all due respect, Prefect —" How did Twigs know this man was a Prefect? "— I'd rather take an action that can give us a chance at survival. For all we know, Life Ring II may not be in a position to help."

Laughing, Prefect Froth replies, "Are we really going to listen to a little child?"

"You don't have to listen to us," Enkidu responds. "You can stay here and die. I would be okay with that." I can't tell if Enkidu is joking and neither can Prefect Froth. They both glare at each other.

Twigs adds, "Prefect Gray is the reason we are all here in this dilemma. Up until a few days ago I was set on looking out for me and planning my own escape. The irony is not lost on me that it was Avi who saved me. If not for him all the test subjects in our facility would have died. It was Avi's guard, Syd, who carried me on his back and to safety. I've never been so scared in my life." He pauses and hangs his head. "Nor so ashamed. In the end I am inclined to follow those who never gave up on me: Amy, Enkidu, Avi, and Syd. If they think we should go to the mountains, then that is where we should go."

I jump in. "This is no longer a dictatorship, nor a democracy. It is survival and everyone is responsible for themselves at this point. No one will make any of you come with us. If you want to build your wells or fix your communicators, you are welcome to do that. As for Syd, Amy, Twigs, Enkidu, and I, we are going to the mountains. Those who want to join us are welcome to come."

A silence spreads amongst the group. Without any objections, I take it that we are all about to head to the majestic mountains, taking our chances with whatever we may face on the way there.

As the suns set we begin our journey to the mountains, realizing it is better to travel at night. We won't have to deal with heat exhaustion and burning. Amy, Twigs, and Enkidu's pico-tech seems to give them a serious advantage, as Prefect Gray described. The rest of us, however, cannot manage the temperature during the day. All of the survivors travel with us, including four prefects from other facilities. It is becoming more and more apparent how unaware they were of everything Prefect Gray was doing. I wonder what happened to Prefect Gray. If it was Zuri behind her in the facility I can only imagine she got what was coming to her.

"I am sorry," Twigs approaches me from behind as we tread through the evening sands, "for being such a brat. I misjudged you before. Having been in such a state of despair, I didn't see any way out. Also, unlike the others, I saw what was happening in the facility. People weren't returning home. They were disappearing one by one, and every night I went to sleep worrying I'd be the next to go. It hurt too much to get close to anyone just to have them whisked away." He holds out his hand to shake mine. It seems kind of awkward but I remind myself he's just a kid and probably doesn't know what else to do. I shake his hand and he adds. "Thank you for not giving up on me."

"Don't mention it," I say, joking. "I'll have to be honest, though. It was tough not to give up on you."

"I know. I can be a challenge sometimes. It is what my mom used to always say." His face turns somber upon remembering his mom and knowing she is gone now.

"I am sorry for your loss, Twigs." I put my hand on his shoulder. "I am sorry, too," he responds.

"For what?"

"For the Ai back in the facility." He explains. "I basically killed it. That is when I realized how fragile life is. It could have been me in that stained glass. I'm responsible for that life. Someday I want to find a way into Apollyon and save the Ai I sent there."

I tell him, "Maybe someday you will. For now we just need to worry about staying alive."

We walk side by side a few more moments, enjoying a comfortable silence and understanding. I watch Enkidu and Amy, near the back of the group. They seem to be conversing. No doubt Enkidu is attempting to cheer her up.

To our right I hear Syd speaking with one of the survivors. From what I overhear, she was a test subject at another facility and went to the same college as Syd.

"I'm going to go see how Amy is," Twigs comments, breaking off.

I nod and smile, watching him go back to Amy. Enkidu peels away as he sees Twigs approaching. It is interesting how quickly Enkidu opened up to Syd and me but how he refuses to do the same with a nine-year-old boy. Twigs must have really rubbed him the wrong way during their time together.

From time to time I glance back and see Amy's demeanor improving. Speaking with Twigs, she even smiles and appears to giggle from time to time. It is a gloom-piercing change to see a grin on her face after all that has happened, though I know it is a temporary one.

Glancing back to Syd, he continues to chat away. Ahead of us the mountains still seem so far away. Behind us the camp from the previous day is gone. The unfamiliar stars hold their place in the sky and we continue to march. The windless night allows us time to gather our thoughts and understand our own place in all that has happened, and I enjoy feeling, like there is a purpose and significance to what we do. The magnitude of our actions will define our place in history...if there is a history for our kind. Will humanity be forgotten with the destruction of its planet, a footnote in a universe which was host to many greater races?

A fight breaks out behind me, accompanied by shouts and yells. I turn to see two men arguing over a canteen. By the time I get there, Syd has broken up the scuffle and is lecturing the two men. "Stop it, you two! Any sound could attract a predator and we don't know what all is out here... blimey, bunch of idiots," he continues with a grunt.

I no longer see Twigs with Amy when I glance back. She's by herself and I decide to check on her. Slowing my pace, I allow myself to fall back in the ranks of our company. Falling in line with her, I say, "Twigs seems to have done a lot of growing up".

She forces a smile. "He had to but he should have never been in a position where he had to."

I agree. "None of us should have been in the positions we were put in. I'm sorry for my role in it. I shouldn't have played Prefect Gray's game for as long as I did. I shouldn't have let her do what she did to Lazarus."

Amy's eyes look into mine, but the moment is cut short — her eyes growing big and darting over my right shoulder.

"What's that?" Amy is focused on a series of dust clouds in the distance. Looking around I see that they come from all directions, no doubt on a path straight for us.

CHAPTER SEVEN
PREDATORS IN THE DARK

As the dust clouds move closer I am unable to locate their source. But deep down my dread grows. I know what they are — sand worms. The ground beneath our feet begins to shake, knocking some people off balance. In the distance, I can make out their writhing torsos breaking through the sand like a shark's fin in the ocean.

"Everyone remain calm! No sudden movements!" I shout. Remembering Lazarus and his attack, it is hard to maintain composure, but I realize panic will only draw attention to me. Looking around, I see some of the others have listened: staying calm, moving closer together in a tight circle, and remaining quiet.

Other individuals succumb to their fear and make a break for it, running toward the mountains, which are at least a day away. Helpless to intervene I watch, cringing as one of the dust trails breaks from its original trajectory and toward a person. The dust stops ten to twenty feet short of the individual. Unable to turn away, I know the worm has dived deeper to build momentum in what will certainly be a deadly attack. Then like a breaching great white, it shoots out of the sand, devouring the person in one swift motion. Seeing such a massive creature move so fast is a terrifying experience. Upon landing it easily slides back into the sand, as if it were mere water.

Out of the corner of my eye, another member of our group breaks off, and my heart drops when I see who it is — Twigs.

"Twigs, what are you doing? Stop running!" I begin to panic.

Keeping my eyes on the worms, I notice not one but three trails turn to Twigs and dart toward him. With the physical benefit of picotechnology, he sprints at a speed beyond a person's natural capacities. Hope enters my heart that his newfound agility will somehow help him to survive his foolishness. He's smarter than this. Why did he leave the group like that?

Just as my hope for his survival surfaces, another dust trail appears directly in front of him. He freezes, turns to face us, and shouts, "Run! Get out of here!" All four worms lunge simultaneously. Instead of waiting to become a meal, I see a light glowing in his open hand and he aims his palm at the ground. In that instant a ball of energy explodes, engulfing the ground and enshrouding Twigs and the worms in a mushroom cloud of debris. The worms' bodies flail and are silent. Smoke and burning ash rise into the night sky.

"No!" I hear Amy scream. Before she can run toward Twigs and expose herself, I cut her off and hold her back.

"You can't help him," I tell her. "He's gone."

The remaining predators have begun to circle, and get closer with each pass. I am about to resign myself to the icy grip of death when I hear a sound in the distance.

The drumming of hooves beat in rhythm as I hear the sound again — a horn. What looks to be an organized cavalry rushes toward us, joining the fray. They look humanoid but are much taller, veiled in cloaks. What are they? They are lean and tall. The animals they ride resemble horses but are much bigger.

The worms scatter as the riders weave between them. Some use long lances to keep the worms at a distance. Others begin summoning spikes of ice out of thin air and shoot the newly formed projectiles into the ground, the sand turning red once they've met their mark. Whatever they are, they have hunted these worms before. And what are those projectiles? I can only describe them as magic — but not anything I've yet seen by done by pico-tech in humans.

Light can be seen in the distance, signaling that a new dawn is on the horizon. The worms are pushed back into the desert. They seem to know these unknown figures as their enemies and retreat.

Our safety obtained, one of the riders trots over to us. I can't seem to make out a face behind the long cloak. The only distinguishable features they share are horn-like protrusions coming from the tops of their heads. They all seem to be carrying long staffs, which look to be made from sand worm tusks. A voice comes from behind the veil. "Who is your leader?"

How is it that they can speak English? Everyone remains silent, probably still in shock from all that has happened, most recently the worm attack. Some mourn the loss of their friends. Amy has tears in her eyes as I step away from her and assume the responsibility of leadership. "I am. I will speak on our behalf. What..."

"There is no time to talk. You will follow us to our village where it will be up to our council to determine your fate."

The formation his cavalry takes indicates his demand is more than a polite request. What he really means to say is, you are coming with us whether you want to or not.

CHAPTER EIGHT
A DESTRUCTIVE RACE

Majestically simple, the town we enter into is unique: rustic mud-brick buildings with a combination of windmill and waterwheel designs. Colorful roofs are shaped into domes, giving a bright complexion to an otherwise plain color scheme. The gem-colored tops glisten even in these dawning hours.

As we pass through an entryway cut into a protective outer wall, I see purple and yellow flags moving in the wind.

The edge of town is filled with farms and orchards, causing me to wonder what could ever grow in the desert. The soil appears surprisingly fertile and the trees and plants are healthy. Unfamiliar animals with thick wooly coats graze in the distance.

The population density increases as we move toward the center of the town, and the buildings become slightly larger but there doesn't seem to be much disparity in terms of wealth distribution. This race, whose pre-adolescent children rival myself in height, funnel out of their houses to see us marched into town. The looks they give us as they retreat from their homes are unnerving, ones of both disgust and awe. I'm not sure of what to expect when we finally reach a large building. This must be the town council.

Some black and white canopies are set up as stores along a main street. Moving down the street, I glance down the alleyways and see carts filled with what look to be edible fruits and vegetables, some familiar and some which I have never seen before. I smell the sweet combination of aromas, reminding me of how hungry I really am.

We stop outside the entrance and the others are told to wait outside. They only want to speak with me. The creature in the black flowing cloak dismounts, inviting me to follow him in. We walk into a small chamber with a circular rug in its center. Four pillows are set around the edge of the rug and two of them are occupied, one by someone who seems to be an elder. He wears a white cloth over his head, as the others do, firmly held in place by a gold band wrapping round long spiraling horns. The other is dressed similarly except he is wearing a deep crimson robe with accents of gold.

The red robed one raises his arm, an open palm over one of the empty pillows. I take it as an invitation for me to sit. The guard who brought us here sits in the remaining empty space. After a brief but very uncomfortable silence we begin.

"My name is Volue," the eldest says. He then nods to the one on his right. "You have already met Denom." Turning back towards me he adds, "This is the City of Garrett. We are the Morai. We are charged with its keeping."

"My name is Avi Taylor." I introduce myself. "Avi Taylor, why are you here?" he asks.

"It is a long story," I say. "I'm not sure where to start."

"Start from the beginning," he insists. "We have time."

I do my best to explain Earth, the sequence of events which led to its destruction, and how we came to be on Mythe. They listen intently, not once trying to speak.

When I finish, Volue says, "You must pardon our reactions to seeing you. By being here, you are fulfilling an ancient prophecy, believed around this world. It has been said that the return of humans to Mythe is a sign, signaling the beginning of the end of days. As such, you may understand our reaction."

"Return?" I ask. "What do you mean by humans 'returning' to Mythe?"

"It is...as you would say...a long story. About ten thousand years ago, your kind instigated a genocide on a particular race here on Mythe and were subsequently banished to the far reaches of our universe, as far away from intelligent life as possible. Your former Earth. We would have noticed your return earlier, had you settled in this region of the desert, a much more habitable section of the Forgotten Dunes. Instead your kind established a base, unknown to us until now, in the dangerous Living Sands surrounding the mountains. Our species avoid that area at all costs due to the variety of savage and poisonous creatures that call it their home. Drawn to the mercurial.

"We also are responsible for keeping watch over these lands. They were once the home of humans. Ensuring that the memory of your time here was destroyed and protected from future generations on Mythe. If humans ever did return, we suspected they would appear here. Which, as it seems, you have."

"Why did you save us?" I ask.

"We need answers. Answers that may help us understand the consequences of these events. If anyone outside of the Morai were to discover you, the planet would surely fall into chaos and entropy."

He notices my disbelief and says, "Something that troubles us greatly is how the few of you from this facility were able to reenter our atmosphere. There is only one way that you would have been able to do so — but how was that possible? For I am sure the attempted reentry for the rest of your kind did not go unnoticed. We must move quickly to ensure that Mythe does not connect those dots. For the sake of all of us." He pauses.

"However, I fear we may be too late. A darkness has been growing over the Mercurial Mountains. The mountains to which you were heading are sacred and guarded by powerful ancient stone golems, the sworn protectors of the mercurial. They are generally a peaceful race — but that has changed upon your arrival. Storms now rage above the mountains: an omen and a sign. We believed something was wrong and that suspicion was confirmed last night when the golems attacked one of our scout parties.

"It is to our great sadness we must admit the golems have a new leader. Our scout reported seeing a floating woman, which we have called the White Witch, journeying to the mountains. We can only suspect that this witch now controls the golems and cannot challenge her. Her powers are unmatched to anything we have ever seen. You brought upon this world a great threat and it will now be your responsibility to purge us of it."

I ask, "If you cannot defeat the golems and this White Witch, then what chance do you think we have against them?"

"That is not of our concern. Unfortunately, you leave us in a difficult position. Rid the mountains of this witch or we will rid Mythe of you."

CHAPTER NINE
CHOICES

Back with Syd, Enkidu, and Amy, I explain. "Zuri is alive. They encountered her journeying to the mountains and spoke of her incredible power. They have been calling her the White Witch. She's taken control of a powerful race of stone golems within the Mercurial Mountains. They've demanded we send someone to kill her before the rest of Mythe discovers our presence. They will not help us."

"Oh, is that all?" Enkidu jests, sarcasm saturating every syllable. "That doesn't sound too tough."

"They seem to be alright with us being here as long as no one can discover us. I reasoned with them to allow us to live in the city indefinitely until we can figure out what to do next. They will place a magical enchantment called a 'void' around the city, hiding us from the outside world," I explain, fearing what I have to say next. "This creates a problem for whomever we send after Zuri. They will never be able to find their way back."

I take a breath and continue. "The Morai will remain outside the void."

"Well, that doesn't sound so terrible," Enkidu says.

"Huh?" Amy asks.

"I'm volunteering to go."

"I won't let you go alone," Amy protests.

"Amy," he says, "do you really think that I would do this alone? I may be crazy but come on...I met some new friends on our way here that I am sure will be more than happy to come with me. As long as I don't mention stone golems, sand worms, or an all powerful witch, that is." He snickers.

"What if you don't succeed?" she asks. "I'll never see you again."

He smiles. "Don't be so certain of that. I'm not going to go down without a fight." He places his hand on Amy's shoulder.

She embraces him, tears forming in her eyes.

"There is one more thing," I say.

"What is that?" Syd asks.

"The Morai have a final request of our stay here. They will wipe the memories of everyone but ourselves. They don't want anyone to leave the void or even know life exists beyond it. If anyone were to remember Earth or the history of our people, it would jeopardize everything. We have no choice but to remain inside the void."

"Well, what are we waiting for?" Enkidu steps forward. "Let's not give her any extra time to become more powerful. That's the last thing I need."

We all say our goodbyes and wish him luck. It is hard to say them, knowing what dangers lie ahead. They make their way to the edge of town as the void, like cascading water over a dome, veils us from the outside world. Enkidu and his group can be seen no more.

CHAPTER TEN
A REGRESSIVE PROGRESSION

Three months have passed now. Amy, Syd, and I remember the truth. Everyone else is oblivious to the lives they lived before Garrett and are unaware of the planet which was their home. The irony there is that we really are home. So far, all they remember is that they are from this small town, one that is self sustaining, with no reason to ever leave. Those of us who know the truth keep the secret and guard it, knowing that our livelihood depends on no one ever leaving the void.

It is interesting to see families form among the strangers who just met, but have in their own minds known each other their whole lives. The most common occupation of the people is farming and they have quickly mastered the art of irrigation. When the void was established, it also created a new world inside. Green rolling hills in the distance replace sand dunes, waterfalls cascade down mountains, replacing bare rocks. I still appreciate this new oasis, even if it is all a lie.

Syd has taken to his new role as mayor quite well. He has fallen in love with a pretty woman from another facility. They seem to be very happy together. Similarly, Amy and I have begun to build our own relationship.

A year passes since we established Garrett, crops are growing, and soon it will be our first harvest. From time to time we — those who know the truth — wonder about the happenings outside of town. Enkidu and his mission come up regularly in our private conversations. We have no idea if he was successful in his mission. We can only hope.

Amy also thinks often about the fate of her brother Lazarus, still hoping she may be able to save him someday. The last thing Volue said to me before setting up the void was to wait for a sign. We are hoping that sign comes soon, so we would be able to leave Garrett and find out those answers for ourselves.

Amy's aptitude for magic grows and so has her relationship with me. We have been together for almost a year, now. It has been one of the best years of my life. Finding her has made me realize how lucky we are despite the circumstances. I finally got up the courage to ask her hand in marriage, and, after an elaborate scheme, I proposed. Her answer was a kiss.

Nine months have gone by since the wedding. Shortly afterwards, we had our first child. Amy insisted we name her Phoenix, after Enkidu's late daughter. I couldn't agree more. It felt like the perfect way to pay respect for one of our dear friends.

We all knew the significance of Phoenix's birth. She was the first human child born on Mythe in an age.

SPOILER ALERT

The third and final act of this book is the entire storyline for our upcoming game. Please do not continue reading if you would rather have the story unfold for you in the the game instead of the novel.

Otherwise, journey onward!

....

The ground jolts beneath me, shooting me forward to land face first into the sand. The shaking intensifies. I look back to see a giant swirling vortex has appeared as if a plug has just been pulled from underneath the sand. And in that moment, emerging out of the center of the vortex, he appears. Shooting into the sky, Lazarus lunges upward. The winged beast has no time to react as it is swallowed whole right before my eyes. Lazarus falls back to the ground, releasing a massive explosion of energy and sand, tossing me uncontrollably into the air. I crash back into the ground.

....

ACT THREE
THE DAUGHTER

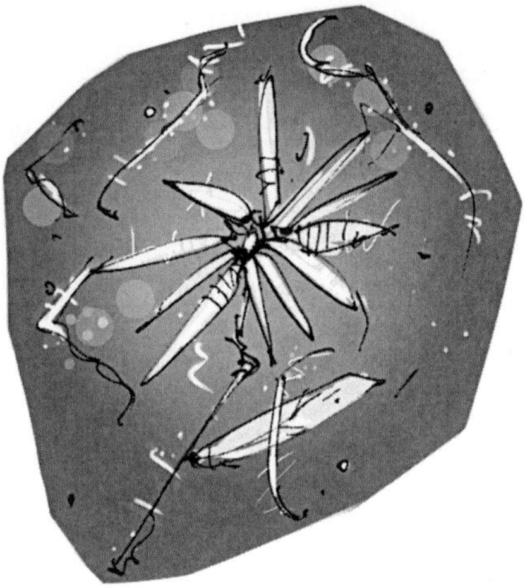

CHAPTER ONE
A HAPPY PLACE

Garrett is my home. The lush green fields and farms provide us plenty to eat: manzaps, zanarots, and melons. The livestock, mostly cows and chickens, is enough to provide cheese and meat for the one hundred and fifty people who live here...I wish there were more kids. I was raised alone by my father. My mother died during childbirth. He says I look just like her. Messy shoulder length brown hair with matching eyes.

Cut grass, bushes, and pine trees infuse the town with deep shades of jade and emerald, extending out from the town square and into the countryside, where fields become rolling mounds. A river encircles the town, creating a natural border for Garrett. Crashing waterfalls shadow over us on the northern bank. They are called Lion Falls because they always seem to be roaring. We never cross the river, no one does. Endless trees are on the other side of it in every direction.

That is where they say the monsters wait, anxiously ready to devour any who trespass into their domain. But I don't believe in monsters.

Our houses are colorful constructs, creatively painted and designed, with domes for roofs and circular, exterior walls. Windmills and waterwheels generate electricity. Papa continues to invent things which aid our town in everyday chores.

Speaking of chores, mine for today is to clean the chicken coop. The coop is a simple construct of two wooden boxes placed side by side with one slightly taller than the other. A triangular roof protects the interior, allowing rain to harmlessly fall away. It usually rains every day but it hasn't for nearly a week.

Sticking my head inside the coop and looking left and right, I wrinkle my nose and instinctively draw back. It smells awful today, definitely worse than usual. Come to think of it, the coop always seems worse than usual on such a beautiful day. I'd rather be out playing and watching the stray, fluffy cumulous clouds float by overhead. Maybe I'll have time to play in the afternoon.

Sighing, putting on leather gloves, grabbing my waste bucket and scoop, and forcing myself into the tiny structure, I begin to remove the bedding material and lay fresh hay. My work is halted when I hear my name in the distance.

"Phoenix!" a familiar voice calls.

Retreating from the stink of the coop and into some fresh air, I turn to the sound of the voice and see her approaching in the distance. "Vida!" I shout. "Thank goodness you're here. What are we doing today?"

"Shouldn't you finish cleaning the coop? I can help," she volunteers.

"I've finished most of it. I can do the rest this afternoon," I insist, running over to her through the field of wispy, tall grass and asking her again. "Let's do something fun today. It is so pretty out!"

"I think we should go to the southern bank," she suggests.

"The southern bank? Why?"

"Didn't you hear?"

"No, hear what?" I ask.

"Old lady Hectate told the town council she saw a monster in the woods there. I was hoping we could catch a glimpse for ourselves," she explains.

"You aren't scared?" Her ambition surprises me. I'm usually the one who pushes us to do dangerous things, in spite of her protestations.

"Monsters never come across the river, right? It should be safe." She pauses. "Right?"

"I guess so. I mean, no one has ever actually proved they've seen a monster before. How do we even know there really are monsters? And if they are real, how do we know they can't swim?" Her shoulders tense and I realize my comment about swimming frightens her. To put her mind at ease I add, "Let's go but don't expect to find anything. You know how Hectate is. She probably made it all up."

"Yup," she contemplates. "That doesn't mean we shouldn't go see for ourselves. What do we have to lose?"

"Right," I say. I put down my tools, take off my gloves, and we begin the trek to the southern edge of town.

Vida wears a purple cotton dress. It extends down just past her knees. Her short red hair is braided and her green eyes shine beneath the bright, morning sun. I am glad my dad never makes me wear dresses. They are too restricting. Plain, black, cotton slacks and a matching blouse are fine with me.

A small dirt path connects all the homes and buildings of Garrett. We follow the path around the edge of the city to where it turns south and we continue toward the southern bank. The path fades as we reach rolling hills and the grass becomes shorter. As the river takes its place on the horizon, we begin to notice brilliant bright flowers, boasting every color of the rainbow. A light, warm breeze blows against my face and whistles in the cattails along the bank. The environment is beautiful but what is beauty without adventure?

I run up behind Vida and poke her shoulder and shout, "You're it". And then I sprint ahead. I hear her chasing behind me. Eventually, I let her catch me. She is breathing heavily when she finally does and I am hardly winded.

After tagging me, she continues on ahead and I give her a head start. I am about to chase after her when I hear something snap and yell, "Stop! Wait one second." A large flower on the ground near my feet has been stomped into the earth and uprooted. I can't help but bend down to look at the broken flower. Two of its white petals break off in my hand as I scoop it up.

"What is it?" Vida asks.

"Just come," I insist. I run my pointer finger along the edges of the delicate plant. As I pull my hand away the stem begins to twitch.

"Whoa!" Vida catches my shoulders. "How do you do those kinds of things? I want to learn!"

"I can't explain it," I tell her. "I have always been able to do these sorts of things."

"Look at it now!" exclaims Vida, pointing at the flower.

The flower begins to glow slightly and flies out of my hand, falling onto the earth. Vida lets out a squeal of delight as she falls backward into the grass.

"Vida, hold these." I hand her the two remaining petals. I bend over, retrieve the flower and stand back up.

"I'm going to try something," I explain, snatching one of the petals from her hand and holding it to its original place on the flower. Focusing on the flower, I feel a strange connection with it. It is a feeling I've experienced before when I concentrate hard enough. The fading life of the flower connects with me and I understand its pain.

It's gasping. Pushing my mind into the damaged areas of the flower, I can sense the tiniest details of each wound.

As I understand, I apply my will to it, and it begins to repair, beginning with the fallen petal and damaged buds, moving down the stem until every strand of the flower is returned to life, power, and vigor. Taking the final petal from Vida, I attach it to the flower and the healing process is complete. It is only after everything that I notice the petals are no longer white. Rather, they are each a glossy variation of red, yellow, orange, green, purple, and blue.

"You fixed it, and you even made it rainbow flower!" Vida proclaims, her eyes the size of saucers. "You are — so cool."

I laugh. I have never understood why I am able to do such things. As far as I know, I am the only one. Papa tells me that I am special. Exactly what a dad would say, but he has never explained it further.

A sudden gust of wind pulls the newly revived flower from my hand and carries it through the air. "Oh no! Let's catch it!" Vida declares, and we chase behind it, up and down the mounds of green and to the river, the rainbow flower dancing in the wind.

We hold our breath and watch as it is carried just above the water, about to become the calm current's victim at any second. Another gust saves the flower, lifting it up and toward the forest. Awe over takes me. It reaches the forest's edge and slowly vanishes. I don't mean it vanishes into the foliage and branches. Rather, it dissolves, centimeter by centimeter, as a luminescence devours it. The flower is gone.

"Whoa. Did you just see that?" I ask.

"Uh huh." She nods. I'm not sure whether it's fear or awe in her expression. "Where'd it go?"

"I'm...not sure." I squint.

Nervousness in her voice and feigning for the sake of appearing brave, Vida jokes, "Let's find out. I dare you to cross the river."

"Okay," I say resolutely, turning my head to her, making eye contact, and smiling.

"No! It was a joke, Phoenix." She tries to retract. "You don't have to. I was just playing. You know we are not allowed to cross the river! You couldn't, even if you wanted to."

She brings up a good point. How would I cross the river? I walk over to its edge, kneel down, look at the dark blue surface, and dip my hand in, letting the cool flow of the current move around the fingers of my open hand, a refreshing sensation. I'm tempted to jump in and swim across but I don't give in. Papa would make me clean the chicken coop every day for the next three years if I came home wet. We'd be in so much trouble.

But I really want to know what happened to our flower. Why did it just disappear into thin air? There is nothing to use as a bridge, nothing to use to float across, and swimming isn't an option. In the past I've always been able to use the magic in me to heal myself and today I projected that outward and healed the flower. I wonder if I can use my magic to influence other things. Closing my eyes and letting my senses expand outward, I try to recognize the river as a living creature. It is different from the flower, not something struggling to survive but rather something full of life: fish, turtles, and tadpoles. There are smaller organisms, too. Too small to see, I don't know what they are but I do know they are there.

"Phoenix, come on! Let's go. Before someone sees us!" Vida says, starting to panic.

"One second. I want to try something."

Vida begins to counter, but crosses her arms, grunts, and sits by the bank in defiance. I think she wants to see this too.

I put my hand back into the river. I feel a strange tingle in my fingertips, causing me to jump back and open my eyes. Staring at the water, I see something bobbing there. It reflects the sun's rays.

Reaching out, I fish it from the river and hold it for a few seconds. It is piercingly cold and slips out of my grasp. "Ice?" I whisper.

"Phoenix, your hair was glowing," Vida says.

"I'm fine," I insist, and stick my hand in the river again.

This time I keep my eyes open, wishing myself to cross the river. I feel a strange sensation pulling at my fingertips. I keep my hand submerged and watch as the water around it begins to turn to ice. It continues to grow, widening and lengthening until, at last, a sheet is formed, joining one side of the river with the other.

I stand up, look at Vida, and take my first step across. Vida protests. "Oh, Phoenix, this is all my fault. We are going to be in so much trouble."

"It will be fine. No harm done," I say, and begin to walk across. She mumbles and moans under her breath, but I am no longer listening. My attention has turned back to the sheet of ice.

I keep the soles of my feet flat as I inch across the strange, slippery platform. The opposite bank gets closer: four steps away, three steps away...I take a few more deep breaths, and carefully step onto the shore of the opposite bank. I turn back to Vida and shout, "I made it!"

"That's great Phoenix," she humors me. "Can we go now?"

"Not yet," I reply. "I want to find the flower."

I ignore any further protestations and move just inches from where the flower disappeared. There is something there. I can't see it or hear it. But I can feel it in my gut. What is it? With caution, I raise my hand, stretching it out to the spot where the flower had vanished. A spark shoots up from my hand as it contacts some type of force. It feels similar to putting your hand through falling water. Unabated, I continue to reach out and break through. Inch by inch my hand disappearing...But my hand isn't gone. I can feel it...I can still wiggle my fingers.

"Phoenix! Stop it! You're scaring me!" Vida continues to protest, and I continue to ignore.

Letting caution overtake curiosity, I pull my hand back and observe. All my fingers are still attached. "Awesome," I whisper. What is on the other side? I prepare to leap forward through the barrier.

"PHOENIX!" This time it is not Vida but my father's voice. I am in deep trouble.

Back inside our home, I watch as my father paces back and forth across the living room. I sit on a sofa near the front door of our house. Papa's workbench is to the left. What appears to be some new type of lamp is atop its surface. Having gotten used to one new invention after another, I don't pay much attention to it. The current house lamp buzzes overhead, hanging from a chain with a barely noticeable sway.

"You know to never cross the river. What were you thinking? I am so disappointed in you," my father lectures. "People have crossed the river and never come back!"

"There was a flower..." I begin.

He interrupts. "I don't care why you did it. I don't ever want to see you down there again." Glaring, I remain silent. Sitting next to me, his tone softens. "Listen, Phoenix. You know I am only upset because I care so much about you. Something could have happened. You may have been killed. People in town are already talking about your little adventure."

"I don't care about what other people think, Papa," I interject.

"Well, in this case, you should." He adds, "People know that you are special and can do things that they can't explain. You shouldn't be drawing too much attention to yourself."

"Why am I special?" I ask, hoping that this time I may get a straightforward answer.

He pauses. "You know that I don't understand it anymore than you do. You said there was a flower?"

Papa is stubborn and I have a feeling that he isn't being completely truthful with me. "Vida and I were playing down by the river. I stepped on a flower. I fixed it and then the wind carried it away."

"What do you mean you fixed it?"

"It was broken, its petals torn off." I pause. "I put them back on and fixed it."

"You healed something else, not just yourself?"

"Yes," I say, not sure why this is such an important question.

His eyes widen. Is he surprised? Afraid? Regaining his composure, he says, "Go to your room. Tomorrow you will have extra chores as punishment for your actions today."

"But tomorrow is the town fair!" I object.

"You'll want to start them early then, if you want to go. Now, off to your room. I'll let you know when dinner's ready."

I stomp from the sofa into my adjacent bedroom. My room is small, a bed against the far wall, a four-pane window above it. Throw pillows line the left wall, while I have a bench for writing along the right. There is a bookshelf near the door.

I make my way to it and grab a book to read while I wait to be released from exile. Jumping onto the bed, I bounce and examine the book cover. It reads 'Riddles for a Rainy Day'. The book has always been one of my favorites. Flipping through the pages, I try to find a unique one...one that I haven't read or don't remember the answer to.

I spend the next hour flipping through and answering riddles out loud. I close the book and lay my head on my pillow, hungry for dinner. I can't stop thinking about returning to the river.

The suns set, leaving the blue moon to reflect their light down upon Garrett. I finish dinner and make my way back to my room. I lean against my window. Outside I can hear some movement, the townspeople finishing some last-minute duties before retiring for the evening. As the town becomes quieter, my excitement becomes greater, knowing soon I'll be able to return to where I lost the flower and discover what is on the other side of the mystical wall. I have to know the answer.

As my father and other townsfolk slip off into the solace of slumber, my mind races and my heart accelerates. Rolling back and forth in the bed, I consider what punishment Papa may come up with if I get caught. So I come up with a simple solution to convince my conscience that what I am doing is right. Don't get caught!

Silence overtaking the town, I continue to wait. Fifteen minutes go by and then thirty. After an hour I decide it is finally safe. Inch by inch I slide open the bedroom window, slipping out into a cloudless, windless night. Soft grass cushions my bare feet, tickling my toes, while I sneak through the dark to the southern edge of town. I once again reach the river bank. I stick my hand into the water and create an ice bridge and inch across to the other side. Surprisingly, it was much easier to create this time around.

The barrier is waiting there for me, silent and tempting. I know it could be dangerous, even deadly, but curiosity and determination drive me, bringing me to inches from it. I have a feeling that I may find some answers on the other side. Taking one final deep breath and closing my eyes, fingers crossed behind my back, I take one more glance at my familiar town and step forward.

The water sensation spreads around me as I move through it. I open my eyes and am met by a new world. No longer am I surrounded by lush green but rather by dead tones of tan, beige, yellow, and brown. It is desert sand glowing under the moonlight. I immediately begin to panic. Human bones. Skeletons lie just in front me. Were these the people who crossed the river and never came back? Will this be my fate too?

I hear the sound of thunder. My attention moves to a storm brewing above a mountain range in the distance. Each blaze of light dances across the desert sand and mountain rock, slowly growing in intensity and size. Their color is white initially but then it shifts to orange, pink, yellow, and purple.

Before I have time to scream, a flash of white blinds me. My vision changes to a dreamlike state. I find myself staring at the shifting lights in the sky above the mountains. Suddenly, I begin to fly, as if someone, or something, is pulling and guiding me there. I fly over the sand and can see a floating island. A large structure is atop it but before I can make out any detail there is another shift, and I am shooting down toward the desert floor.

A squeal escapes me. Before slamming into the desert waves, I pull up, continuing to fly across the sand's surface, up and down dunes. Glowing light shoots out of the mountain tops as worms, gigantic worms, breach in and out of the dunes in front of me. I dart around them, over them, and under. These worms are massive, with menacing tusks protruding out of their mouths like venomous swords.

I can see what seems to be an entrance to the mountain pass in front of me. Large stone figures guard the narrow passageway. They are about nineteen feet high, thin, with wide headdresses and glowing eyes.

I freeze at the top of the mountain. A final burst of purple light and a face is there, nose to nose with me. She's beautiful, with white hair and colorless eyes to match. Beauty transforms into terror as I realize her eyes have no pupils and the blood under her skin illuminates her haunting face.

Staring into my eyes, a twisted smile spreads across her face. "We finally meet." The vision abruptly ends.

I fall backwards from shock. I find myself flying back towards Garrett. The water sensation returns as I pass through the barrier again and fall into the river. I swim to the other side and lie on my back staring at the stars. Who was she? What did any of that mean? I wonder. One thing is for sure. I'm going to have to tell my father and I know he isn't going to like it.

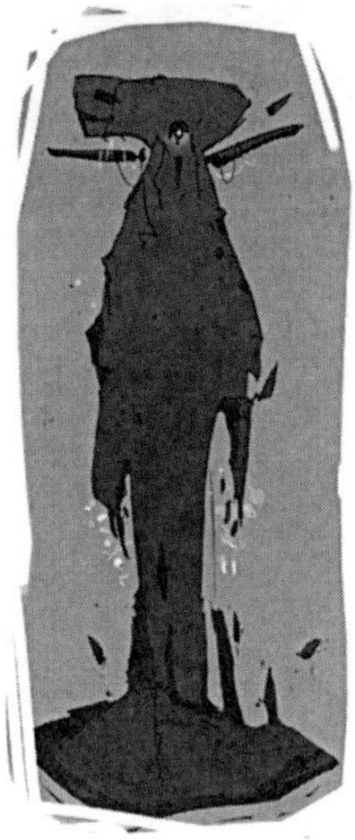

CHAPTER TWO
REMEMBERING

I wasn't able to sleep that night. The next morning I finish my chores in record time, all the while thinking of how to tell my dad about the vision. I need to tell him, but how? For the time being he seems preoccupied with getting ready for the fair.

Leaving our home and beginning our journey to the town square, I try to muster up the courage to tell him but no words escape me. I know it would break his heart if he knew what I had done.

We arrive at the carnival. The town square has been decorated in bright lights, and different games are set up along its edges. Cheerful music is playing. A man with a food cart is set up near the intricate fountain in the plaza's center.

A small tremor shakes the ground, barely noticeable aside from the slight vibration of water in the fountain. I look around to see if others noticed but they seem not to have, too busy playing games and enjoying the festivities. I almost convince myself it was imagined, until I glance over to my dad.

A worried expression on his face, he asks, "What's wrong with you today? You're awfully quiet."

"I am, Papa," I confirm. "Did you feel that?"

"I did..." His voice trails off.

Vida's familiar voice interrupts. "Phoenix, you made it! See, Dad, I told you they would come." Looking towards where her voice is coming from, I see her father trailing behind: a stocky man with a large red mustache. "I'm so glad you are here!"

"Me, too!" I agree, especially considering all the chores I had to finish to be able to come. "What do you want to do first? Have you tried any of the games yet?"

Vida answers my question. "Nope, we just got here, and I was waiting for you."

Vida's father catches up with her and I hear my dad say, "Hello, Syd. Good to see you."

He responds, "Likewise," glancing down at us, Syd continues, "Why don't you girls run along and play?" I see our fathers' demeanors change; they both are concerned. No doubt they are going to talk about the events of yesterday. Maybe now would be a good time to tell him?

"Let's go!" Vida grabs my arm, and capers with me over to the game area.

"There are so many games to choose from! My dad really likes that one. It used to be his favorite," she suggests.

"Sounds great," I agree. I commit to telling my dad on the way home from the fair.

Playing one game after the next, I get up the courage and confess to Vida. "Vida, I went back last night."

"Went back where?" Her tone turns serious.

"The place where the flower disappeared," I explain. "I went through the barrier and saw what was on the other side."

"Huh? What did you see?" Her eyes are large. "How were you able to come back?"

Not wanting to relive the experience, I reluctantly answer. "Desert...human bones...worms...mountains, and..." I pause, considering whether or not to bring up the vision of the woman in the mountains.

She considers my words and her tone darkens. "What? That sounds terrible! Are you sure it wasn't just a bad dream?"

"I know it was real," I reply.

She responds, "And your dad, did you tell him? What did he think about it all?"

"I snuck out and didn't tell him," I admit. "I know I should, but I am afraid to tell him. Any ideas?" I solicit her help.

She's about to answer when I feel another tremor, this one more violent than the others, knocking some people off their feet, including Vida. A grumble in the earth and groaning in the sky accompany the violence of the tremor. The world around us starts to glow, the sky fluctuating in color as it sparks and seems to melt away. Our entire world is changing right before our eyes.

People begin to scream and fight against the quaking and seek out their loved ones, the sound of panic permeating the town. Helping Vida to her feet, I search for my father. What is going on? I see him and Syd approaching. We run toward them but before we do, the last pieces of the sky give way, shattering into shards of light with the accompanying sound of breaking glass.

Splinters of the barrier begin to fall as magnificent light, fizzling into nothingness. With their destruction, the world around us transforms: green hills to sandy dunes, trees to boulders, and water to sandstone. If not for the houses, nothing would look the same at all.

Confusion is inherent on the faces of the townspeople, who are stunned and unmoving. Attempting to comprehend the situation for myself, I look to my father. In contrast to the other people around me, his face shows clarity. You'd think his understanding would be comforting but it has the opposite effect because understanding is not the only thing I see in his eyes. I also see fear. What is he afraid of? Does he know what is happening? Did this happen because of me leaving last night? Syd is standing next to my father and shares the expression of terror and comprehension.

Vida and I run over to them and Papa hugs me, asking, "Phoenix, are you okay?"

"Yes, Papa," I tell him. "What's happening? What is going on?"

"I'm not completely sure..." Before he can say anything else, we are interrupted by a rumbling. I look in all directions, trying to find the source of the sound. Then I see them. Tall shadows appear on the horizon. They look familiar and I realize they are the stone golems I saw last night, the ones from the mountain. Their stone headdresses sway back and forth in the distance, like upside down pendulums. My father turns to Syd. "Lead everyone to the cave. I will take care of Phoenix and Vida."

Syd nods and shouts over the chaos, "Everyone this way. Hurry!" We follow him to the edge of town where Lions Falls used to be. In place of the waterfall there is a cliff with a small cave at its base. Before entering the cavern I turn back to look at the stone giants and see that they are approaching fast. Some people aren't going to make it into the cave before they get here, I tell myself. My heart drops when I see Vida has fallen to the ground.

Turning back I run for her but my father stops me, ordering, "No Phoenix! Follow Syd. I'll get her."

Rushing into the opening in the cliff side, I find myself in the maw of a strange tunnel. It goes further back but Syd stops us just beyond the entrance. I see a mechanical chair with arm straps, bags full of grain, a small well, and a collection of unfamiliar objects. Syd runs to a gun which hangs from the wall. He grabs it and charges back outside the cave.

I slide behind him and follow him out the cave. "PAPA!" I yell, as one of the stone golems wraps its fingers around my father, lifting him into the air and turning to carry him away. Syd points the gun at the golem and shoots. Balls of plasma slam against the monster's stone hide. Syd shoots again but the missiles dance harmlessly across it. I see others are being swept away in a similar manner.

"Daddy! Help!" Vida's voice sounds among the chaos. Searching for her, I see her, on the ground and crawling toward us. Syd sees her too, and bounds over to her, using his weapon to keep stone monsters at bay. Cradling her in one arm he lifts her, continuing to fend off enemies as he returns. One of the golems pursues us and reaches into the cave to grab me as Syd pulls a lever. A wall slams down, sealing us safe in the sandstone mountain side.

"Vida!" I stare at her as Syd lowers his daughter to the ground. "Is she okay?" I hurry by her side, dropping to my knees. "Are you okay?" I lay my hand on her shoulder, careful not to hurt her any worse than she is. Cuts and bruises cover her swollen body.

She coughs. "I'm sorry about your dad...They got him."

"Don't worry about that, now. Are you okay?" I ask. The optimist in me is hopeful for a positive answer; the pessimist in me is doubtful of such an outcome. I can already see a trail of blood escaping out her mouth and running down her cheek.

"I'm fine," she whispers weakly, unable to move. Then her eyes slip shut.

"The flower," Syd says.

"What?" I ask.

"She said you used magic to heal the flower." He begs, "Please, Phoenix, can't you do something for her?"

Why hadn't I thought of that? Closing my eyes, I try to expand into Vida's body. Beginning with where my hand touches her shoulder, I move down toward the heart but before I can reach it, something blocks me. It is like a black wall encircling my consciousness, pushing me out. I try again and this time I can't even connect with her. "I...I can't." I admit defeat. Why isn't it working? "Is there anything else we can do?"

I watch Syd's eyes shift over to the chair and back to his daughter. He says abruptly, "There is one thing." A single tear escapes his eye. "I can save her but it may be kinder to let her go."

I answer, "What do you mean? If you can save her, we have to do it!"

"Please, Dad," Vida coughs, her eyes still closed. "I don't want to die."

"She won't last much longer," I observe. "What do you need me to do?"

Syd sighs, lifting his daughter in his arms and moving over to the strange chair. He straps her wrists and waist down, runs a wire from the base of the chair to a mechanical arm, and places a ring from his finger between its claws.

"Phoenix, give this to Vida," he says, handing me a syringe filled with a strange liquid metal. He notices my hesitation.

"Phoenix, now!" he commands. I stick the needle into Vida's arm and push the liquid into her veins. I take the syringe out.

"Stand back," he says, moving to a panel on the wall. I hadn't noticed it before. It looks like glass but beneath his touch it begins to glow, different shapes on its surface. He navigates them, pushing one after another and causing a beep with each tap of his finger.

With the final beep the chair blazes to life, a powerful white light engulfing it. Vida moans at first, her body twisting from one side to the other. Her face contorts and her eyes open. They are hollow and lifeless, rolling from one side to the other. What is he doing to her? The twisting turns to convulsions as her body slams and pulls against her restraints. Her mouth opens as if to scream but no sound comes out. Then her convulsing stops.

Syd slowly makes his way over to the mechanical arm, releasing the ring from it. His body shakes and his tears flow, unrestrained and full of pain.

"You killed her," I squeak, sadness and anger in my voice. "How could you do that to her?"

"I did the only thing that could save her," Syd says remorsefully. He places the ring in my hand.

"Why would I want..." I begin.

A voice...Vida's voice...interrupts. "Phoenix, is that you? What happened? Where are we?"

The cavern remains in silence. I don't know how much time passes. Maybe it is an hour. Maybe it is five minutes. It seemed like a lifetime. Syd doesn't say much about what happened but he says enough for me to understand that Vida's soul is inside the ring. In the silence I hear her voice, which, based on the others around me, seems that only I can hear.

"Are you in any pain?" I ask her. I can already tell that something has changed in her.

"No, I don't really feel anything at all, to be honest."

An angry voice breaks the silence. "Syd, what is going on? The last thing we remember is talking to the Morai and now all of a sudden we're being attacked by stone golems. Things aren't adding up here."

Syd snaps back, "Prefect, what Avi, Amy, and I did was only to protect us until we heard back from them. It was our only option!"

This is the first time I have ever heard my mom's name mentioned by someone other than my dad. What role did she play in all of this? I listen as Syd explains to the group. Much of it doesn't make any sense. Their memories seem to have been erased. Does that mean they were somewhere else before they were in Garrett? Morai? Life Rings? Earth?

They continue to argue among themselves, the people of Garrett versus Syd. I listen, not being able to understand any of it.

"Sustain our future?" This time it is a woman speaking. "You've condemned us. Now where will we go? What do we do? Are we left to die in this cavern like roaches?"

"The void was supposed to keep us safe." Syd's voice is breaking. How he's kept it together as long as he has is beyond me...after what has happened to Vida. "Something broke it. Somehow the White Witch found us."

"Who is the White Witch?" I ask, fearing his response.

"She lives in a mountain range. She's the one behind the attacks, using the stone golems as her personal army."

My heart sinks and I fall from weakness to the ground. This is my fault.

"I'm not sure how she found us. The void was supposed to veil us from her." The void? That must have been the barrier. It couldn't be more clear. The White Witch found us because of me. I should never have left. My dad and Vida would be okay right now if I'd just listened. Why did I have to be so reckless?

"It's my fault," I confess.

Everyone immediately stops talking.

"What is your fault?" Syd asks.

"The White Witch. I left the barrier last night. I saw her. I'm not sure how, but I did. It is all my fault..."

"So, you're the cause of this?" scoffs the man who Syd called Prefect. "You foolish child!"

The guilt is unbearable. So many people have been hurt from my actions. I don't blame them for being upset. Tears well up in my eyes.

"That's enough, Prefect. Phoenix has been through enough. We have all been through enough," Syd says, making his way over to me. He kneels down by my side.

"Don't cry. Thank you for being honest. What you did is what I would expect any kid your age to do. You were just curious. You didn't mean any harm."

His words lift my spirits a little. I look him in the eye, using my sleeve to wipe away some tears. It still doesn't replace the feeling that I am the one responsible for this mess. My dad, Vida...

"So, what's the plan then? We can't hide in here forever," someone says, breaking the silence.

"We have to confront her. It was our promise to the Morai for allowing us to stay on Mythe, to stay in Garrett. I fear the void collapsing tells us they have become casualties to her bidding. It is the only explanation as to why their magic would fade so suddenly."

Syd looks down at me. I read the expression in his eyes.

"It has to be me, doesn't it?" I stammer, but already knowing the answer.

"Yes. Yes, it does." Syd kneels beside me again. "It is time I tell you the truth about your mother."

Syd and I talk all through the night. He explains to me that my mother didn't die during childbirth but had attempted the same journey that I was about to embark on. He clarifies what I saw happen to Vida, calling her now an Ai. I am grateful to have Syd there to answer all my questions. We grow very close that night, bonding over our mutual losses. By the end I know why I have to be the one to face the White Witch. I am the only one to possess the powers to face her. I am the only one who could potentially save both my mother and father. I am the only one who can save us all.

CHAPTER THREE
AN UNEXPECTED JOURNEY

Syd has offered to help me prepare for the journey. I learn that he had done the same with my mother. We start by re-christening Vida as Luna, symbolizing her new life as an Ai.

"Phoenix," Syd says as I slip on Luna's ring, "I have something for you. Your mother wanted you to have this."

He hands me a beautiful gold necklace. Recognizing its power, I know it to be an Ai.

"This is Artemis. She was your mother's friend. She left this behind in the event that her own journey might not be successful."

For the first time in my life, I feel like my mother is here with me.

Over the next few days, I practice using both of their abilities to amplify my magic. Although I need more time, there is none. It is time for me to go.

I say goodbye to a few of the people and grab my things. Most of them wish me luck and give me a hug goodbye. Syd and I head together deeper into the cave. He has agreed to take me to a secret exit. Now we stride through the narrow tunnels which stretch high on each side. Specks of a mineral glow from the rocky surface. Luna helps me to light our path. Wind and water dripping can be heard in the distance.

Syd asks, "How are you feeling?"

I answer, "Alright, I suppose," unsure of how I really feel.

Syd says reassuringly, "You posses a power that even your mother never had. Remember that when times get tough."

He smiles at me. "You remind me a lot of her. You definitely have her strength. The only time we ever heard from the Morai was to let us know Enkidu was unsuccessful. You were only days old at the time. How hard that must have been for her. She knew it was the only way to save you."

I ask, "Do you think she is dead?"

He stops. "Phoenix, I don't know for sure. That's an answer you may learn once you leave here." He looks at me somberly. "Stay strong when you find the fate of your parents. I can only hope that they are okay, but I am doubtful you will find that."

I know what he says is true.

He continues, "I know you have had to grow up so quickly over the last few days. You are very brave."

We move on. A chirp sounds as we reach a fork in the tunnel.

"What was that?" I ask.

He replies, "Not sure. Let's continue, we're getting close." We take the left passage and walk in silence.

My senses are on high alert after the unfamiliar sound. I jump when the sound returns, adrenaline pumping through my body. It is closer this time. "There it is again," I remark.

I hear the chirping for a third time. This time it is behind us and very close. Shifting to my side, I glance over my shoulder and see it.

Silver fur rippling in excitement, the mouselike creature supports itself on two muscular hind legs, its body the size of a small dog. Small eyes glow a menacing red and its ears twitch. Preparing to leap from an overhead ledge, it bares its teeth.

"Look out!" I shout, as it lunges at Syd. He throws himself into me and we fall. The creature leaps over us, landing on all fours nearby. Collecting myself, I aim my palm at the creature. Energy channels through Artemis and a light arrow slams into the rat, sending it against the wall. It falls unconscious to the ground. Syd helps me up and asks, "Are you okay?"

"I'm fine," I say. "There are probably more of those around here. We need to be alert."

"Right," Syd nods.

We continue on in the tunnel and come across more of the strange creatures without incident. A light appears in the tunnel up ahead.

"Is that the exit?" I question.

"No," he answers, confusion in his voice. "Just be prepared for whatever comes next."

Advancing, I feel a current of air against my face. It grows in intensity the closer we get and the gentle noise it produces turns to a violent howl. Reaching the light, we see that a piece of the tunnel's wall has collapsed into a new chamber. We step through. It is enormous. Running perpendicular with our path, it is perfectly cylindrical. Its diameter must be at least 50 yards.

I look left and right, seeing that it extends both ways as far as my eyes can see. Shimmers of the same light glint all over the walls, illuminating the area.

"What made this?" I ask. "I've never seen anything like it."

"Lazarus," he responds, "the king of the sand worms."

Admiring the cavern a few more seconds, we head back to our path. The light fades behind us and Luna continues to help me light our way. We travel down a few more corridors and then Syd stops and tells me, "We are almost there. Straight ahead, you will see a crevice leading to the outside world. I wish I could continue with you."

I see the sincerity in his eyes. "I know." I smile, saying, "Thank you," and give him a hug. "I am going to miss you. This isn't goodbye. I will find a way back."

I pull away and am about to turn when I hear Luna's voice. "Tell my dad goodbye for me."

I return to face Syd.

"Vida just asked me to tell you goodbye."

Tears forming in his eyes, he breaks eye contact to look at the ground. He breathes deeply. "Tell her I miss her already."

I inform Vida and report back to Syd, "Vida says that she doesn't want you to be sad that our time is over. She wants you to be happy that it happened."

He looks up, sniffling, and smiles. "I will. Good luck, Phoenix."

I nod my head and make for the corner which heads towards the crevice.

Artemis speaks up. "That was really hard. This is it, I suppose."

"Yeah, this is it. We're all by ourselves now. Hopefully we don't get too lost. He said it was just ahead."

She replies, "We'll be alright".

Sneaking through the tunnels, my mind goes blank and my senses switch to high alert. A resolve accompanies me in the darkness, and a fear of what is around the corner. I need to have the confidence to overcome it, no matter what it is.

Navigating through the tunnel system, there are a few branches I explore, some dead ends and others leading me deeper into the dark. I start to feel a current of air against my face and the wailing howl carried therewith. We must be getting close.

Artemis shouts, "Phoenix, look! I think the exit is straight ahead. We're almost there! Just keep going down this tunnel."

We make our way to the crevice and crawl through into the bottom of what looks like a large canyon. Squinting, I can see the sky above me, jagged rock walls extending about 130 feet high on either side of me.

"Well, there's only one direction to go," I say, as I walk down the rocky corridor.

We come to a three-way junction, one pass leading to my left and the other to my right.

"It's a labyrinth," I say, understanding that it is more than possible that this was created by someone or something. It is an unsettling feeling.

I peer down both of the passageways, trying to see any clue that would indicate which way we should go. It seems as if we are about to get the answer to that question.

Through the howling of the wind, a clicking noise emanates from directly behind us. Turning around, I don't immediately see anything. Then, slowly raising my gaze skywards, I see them. About a dozen of the nastiest creatures I have ever seen are making their way down the stone walls towards us. They are arachnid in nature, with hard glinting shells, followed by a long dangerous looking tail.

As I turn to run, I can feel a sharp pain between my shoulder blades, but it doesn't stop me from sprinting down one of the paths as fast as I can. I dart from left to right, my only goal being to get as far away from them as I can. A tingling sensation begins spread down my arm.

"I think we lost them," Luna reassures us.

I come to a stop. Adrenaline wearing off, it feels like my back is on fire. My left arm has gone completely numb. Reaching over my shoulder with my right hand, I can feel the source of my pain. Sharp razor-like barbs are embedded in my skin. Knowing I must hurry to get these things out, I clench my teeth and begin the painful process of pulling them out one by one.

I am sitting on the ground of the labyrinth, with my back against the wall. A pile of barbs is stacked next to me.

"Good thing you're special. I would most certainly have died! Those probably won't even leave a scar." Luna breaks the silence after witnessing the gruesome process.

"Luna is right. You're the only one who probably could have lived through that, as awful as it was," Artemis comments, and continues, "But we should't stay here for much longer. How are you feeling, Phoenix?"

"I'm alright. Let's get going...wherever that is," I say. Running from the arachnids, we could be anywhere now inside this place. We are most definitely lost.

We wander through the seemingly endless corridors. There are so many different ways we can go. Hope begins to fade, replaced by frustration.

"Phoenix, look!" Artemis shouts.

Ahead, I can see what she is referring to. There is a small bright light. It sways back and forth as it makes its way closer to us.

"What is it?" I ask aloud.

"I don't know, but be ready to fight whatever it is," Artemis responds.

I lift my hands and prepare for another encounter. As it approaches, bouncing up and down, I can start to make out details of the strange-looking animal. It is a mix of a mouse and rabbit, with long pointy ears that are connected by a glowing orb directly above its head. It stops, the beady black eyes looking into mine.

"Coo! Coo!" it murmurs.

I don't know what to do. It just stands there, tilting its head, cooing at me from time to time. It turns around and hops a few paces before looking back at me and cooing some more.

"I think it wants us to follow it," Luna suggests.

We follow the strange animal. I name it in my head as an Orbie. Eventually we reach a dead end. It uses its ears to point to a section along the wall. I examine the area and see a small lever. I look back down at the Orbie.

"Coo! Coo!"

I don't know why, but my gut tells me to trust this little animal. I turn the lever.

The wall before us drops into the ground revealing a large chamber with a roaring waterfall ahead. I enter, noticing a large gap separating me from it. Peering over the edge, the water disappears in the infinite darkness.

The Orbie looks up at me and coos before jumping over the chasm and through the wall of water. Where did he go? It obviously wants me to jump as well, but there is absolutely no way I could clear it.

"What do I do?" I ask.

"Don't jump," Artemis offers, sarcastically.

I stand there looking at the wall of water. There must be something behind it that the Orbie wants me to find. But how am I supposed to get over there?

"Phoenix, remember what you did back at the river? With the ice bridge?" Luna suggests.

I think back but that situation was different. I was touching the water, connecting with it to make what I needed. This is a completely different scenario. Or is it? Back at the river, I connected with the environment to make the bridge. Yes, I was touching the water, but was that necessary? Could I do the same thing using my thoughts only?

I kneel to the ground, placing my hands on the cold damp stones. Wishing myself to cross the chasm, I begin feel a familiar sensation at my fingertips. The ground beneath me begins to rumble.

"The ground is moving! You're closing the gap!" Luna excitedly squeals.

Lifting my head, I see the gap has now narrowed to a distance I can easily step over. Amazed at myself, I step through the water.

I am in a small closed chamber. Glints of light dance across the rock walls. In the center, a pedestal stands with a silver object resting on its surface. The Orbie jumps enthusiastically. I reach out and take it.

The first piece I discovered made it clear that there were more to be found. Acquiring the three additional puzzle pieces wasn't a small feat. Miraculously though, we did it. All four pieces fit together perfectly, forming a circular silver coin.

The last trial opens to a passageway that ends with an immense wooden barrier. Embedded in the stone walls are numerous metal gears and chains. Then I see it, a small circular indentation, exactly the size of the coin. We did it.

I reach my hand out to insert the coin in its place, when I feel a sudden excruciating pain. The coin drops to the ground. A barb, about 6 inches long, impales my hand. It is attached to a slimy, writhing, weblike strand. My eyes follow the strand upwards to see a massive arachnid creature straddling the canyon opening high above me.

The barb retracts, pulling me upwards like a fish caught on a hook. My body scrapes along the rocky walls as I am being dragged upwards to the terrifying creature. Regaining my senses, I channel Artemis's power, shooting a light arrow, severing the sinew connecting me to the beast. It howls in pain and I fall to the ground.

I yank the barb from my hand and struggle to my feet as the beast's shadow envelopes me from overhead. I turn to see it descending the canyon walls, using its impressive leg span to suspend itself above me.

Behind its massive body I see a long tail ascend into the air. It is covered by armored plates and ends with two sharp stingers. As its shadow passes over me, it strikes. I roll out of the way just in time to see them make contact where not even a second ago I was lying.

It continues to pummel the ground in quick succession, leaving craters in its wake. I dodge and roll from the relentless attacks, not giving me any time to fight back.

"Do something, Phoenix!" Artemis shouts.

"I'm..." I gasp, as I'm being cut off by another strike, "...trying!"

I hear a familiar sound in the distance. A series of cooing echoes throughout the canyon. Orbies.

The monster seems distracted by the noise, and slowly starts to shift its body away from me. I get a quick glimpse of a small pack of Orbies bouncing up and down and waving their orbs back and forth. It buys into their distraction, chasing after them. I hear the sounds of the Orbies carrying it deeper into the labyrinth.

Finally able to catch my breath, I feel relief and gratitude for the Orbies. If only I could thank them for what they did. I crawl to the fallen coin near the wall.

"Phoenix," Artemis says, gasping, "I don't know if we will be much help if we run into any more danger soon."

"Our energy is drained, just as yours is. We need to find somewhere to rest," Luna adds.

"You're right. Let's hope that this thing doesn't have a brother waiting for us on the other side," I say, reaching down for the coin.

I take a deep breath, close my eyes and place the coin in its slot. The gears and chains around me begin to thunder to life. The wooden barrier begins to lower like a drawbridge away from me. The suns' rays cascade over the bridge as it lowers. The light eventually surrounds me, bringing with it a burning heat. I raise my hand over my eyes to get a better view of what lies ahead.

"Whoa..." Luna says in wonder.

I stand there in awe as my eyes sweep over rolling endless sand dunes. They twinkle like millions of jewels under the two hot suns, like an ocean of living light. The beauty of the setting before me is in sharp contrast to the ominous mountain range lying in the distance. I know those mountains. I have seen them before. That is where I am headed. That is where she waits.

Stepping across the bridge, I glance over its edge. There is a harrowing ravine, the bottom of which I cannot see. The mountain labyrinth extends upward behind me. I reach the edge and step from the wooden planks to the sandy dunes of Mythe.

I journey forward, lazy clouds floating overhead, approaching a large dune. My lips are parched and my mouth dry.

"What's that up there?" I ask, looking at an odd display of vivid colors growing up out of the sand near the top.

"Only one way to find out," Artemis says.

Climbing to the top of the massive dune proves to be a challenge, every step seemingly becoming harder than the next, the suns's unforgiving rays pounding down on me like fists of fire, and the occasional gust of wind embedding sand crystals in my eyes.

I glance up to see a small arrangement of beautiful flowers that are about waist high. Their petals are large and curve up to the sky. A shimmer of something from within the petals catches my eyes.

"Water!" I exclaim, as I run to the nearest one. Lifting the petal to my lips, the liquid enters my mouth. I cannot begin to describe how delicious the water actually is. It fills me with a refreshing sense of hope and life. Each flower holding only a small amount, I move to the next and repeat the process.

Approaching the last flower, Artemis stops me.

"Wait, Phoenix! Look, this flower is oddly different."

I look carefully and notice very small sharp protrusions encircling this particular flower.

"What do you think it is?" I ask.

"Try tossing something near it," Artemis replies.

I grab a rock from the ground and fling it onto the suspicious plant. Not a second passes before it touches the ground and we realize that the sharp protrusions are the teeth of a strange fishlike monster, snapping its jaws shut around the bait. Disappointed, it reopens its mouth and once again sinks beneath the sand, waiting for the next unsuspecting victim.

"I really don't like this place," I state.

"Maybe we'll find someone to help us over there," Artemis suggests.

Not realizing that we had reached the top of the dune, I glance up. Directly ahead I can make out a floating island not far from us, its base an upside down cone of brown dirt and gnarled roots. Its surface appears to be covered in green grass and leafy trees. A stream ends in a waterfall at the island's edge, the water seeming to disappear in midair some twenty feet down. A stone building of some sort — maybe a castle or observatory — could someone be living there?

The island has four massive chains tethering it to the ground below, giving the impression that it would float away like a balloon without them. A cavernous hole in the ground is left in its wake, no doubt where it used to belong.

Going down the dune is much easier than going up, sometimes nearly falling as my momentum carries me towards the bottom. Walking towards the island, I keep my eyes out for any signs of life but don't see anything. How can anyone ever get up there? I approach one of the chains. The thickness of the link is easily three times the size of me. It is the only way I can think to reach the top.

I try to wrap my hands around the hot metal link, but after a weak attempt, my stomach twists as I gaze out over the black hole in front of me. The thought of climbing this chain and falling into the cavernous abyss below makes my legs feel weak. I grunt, give up, and step away from the edge.

Something hard comes crashing down on top of my head, briefly making me see colored lights. My head begins to throb. Rubbing the spot of impact, I open my eyes. In front of me is a rope, dangling and swaying. Looking up, it appears to be tethered high up on the island. Somebody knows I am here.

"If we encounter something, Phoenix, I have regained a little strength but not much," Artemis says.

"Me too. Be careful, Phoenix," Luna adds, with a worried tone in her voice.

I take hold of the rope with both hands and push off from the ground, holding on tightly as it sways back and forth. I begin to climb.

CHAPTER FOUR
A HERMIT IN THE SKY

Climbing the rope, my hands begin to ache and burn. Multiple times I felt that I can't climb higher, but Artemis and Luna's encouraging words keep me going. I take a peek and see that I am not far from the island's edge. I take a big deep breath and pull myself higher.

I begin to grab on to some of the rocks to hoist myself over the edge. A few crumble away, falling below, leaving me dangling helplessly. I feel a firm grip on my wrist, yanking me up onto the island's surface. My face is met with the softness of grass.

"Who are you?" a voice demands.

I brush myself off and begin to stand to face the stranger. He looks as if he is ninety years old. His face is square with a large round nose. His skin is dark from over-exposure to the suns — giving it a leathery texture. He's messy, with tufts of white hair sticking out in all directions. I can see bushy eyebrows that match a long wiry beard. He is wearing some sort of animal skull as a hat.

"My name is Phoenix. What's yours?" I ask politely.

At the mention of my name he leans forward, squinting. He pauses there for a moment. Suddenly he gasps and jumps back, covering his mouth with his hand, the skull wobbling on his head.

"I'm sorry, did I scare you?" I ask, confused.

"You're Amy's daughter." He pauses, stepping closer and lowering his hand. "You look just like her."

"You knew my mother?" I question.

"Oh, yes, very well. We were close friends."

I am not understanding what's going on.

"Who are you?" I ask again.

He slaps his face, shaking his head.

"I'm so sorry. How rude of me. My name is Enkidu. Please, come inside. We have much to discuss." He trots over to a small archway.

I hesitate to follow.

"It's okay, Phoenix, you can trust him. He loved your mother," Artemis says, noticing my reluctance to follow.

Stepping through the entrance, I go into the observatory, beautiful and strange in its own way. It is a wide open area with no floor, just grass continuing to grow inside. I look around and notice the odd placement of doors and windows. Some doors are upside down and several feet above the ground.

"My magic ain't perfect, my dear," Enkidu says, catching me looking around bewildered.

"Please, please, please, have a seat. You must be tired and thirsty. Make yourself at home." He continues, "I'll be back with some tea and water".

I watch him leave the room, struggling to crawl through a small square opening near the ground.

Through a series of grunt and groans he shouts, "Phoenix! Give the old man a push, won't you?"

I walk over and awkwardly start shoving him through. Before I know it, the rest of his body disappears through the hole, followed by a large crashing sound. Did he fall?

"Are you okay?" I shout through the opening, my voice echoing down to Enkidu.

"Yup, just remembered I never got around to putting that floor in. Be up in jiffy!" he calls back.

Suppressing my laughter, I make my way back to the table, and take a seat. I notice a pitcher of water already on the table and pour myself a glass. Looking around and enjoying the refreshment, I feel like I am back home, in a way. Strange objects, animal skeletons, and half-built knick knacks litter the space. It reminds me so much of my dad. My heart sinks.

Before I can dwell too much on my sadness, the room is suddenly filled with dust and debris as Enkidu falls through the ceiling.

"Arrggaaahh!" a sound escapes him as he lands with a thud.

I cough and brush dust from my eyes and make my way over to him. His body lies there motionless. His mouth and eyes open. My stomach jumps into my throat. Is he dead? I kneel down and shake him.

"Enkidu! Are you okay? Please answer me!" I shout. There is no response. I reach back and grab the glass of water off the table and splash the remains on his face.

"Oaoaoaoa!" he gasps, sucking in air.

"I thought you were dead!" I say, lifting him up, beads of water trickling off his beard as he rises.

"No, not dead, just knocked out. Nothing to be worried about! Wait, how'd you get the water?" he asks.

"There was already a pitcher on the table," I respond.

He chuckles, "I should have remembered. But never mind that, let's talk about why you're here, shall we?"

Enkidu and I sit at the table until there is barely any light left on the horizon. Our conversation was overwhelming, my world turned upside down. Everything I knew to be true yesterday was nothing but a facade.

"Alright, it's time to call it a day." He refuses to answer my last question. "Let's get you to bed. You have a long day ahead tomorrow."

I don't argue, and he walks me over to a set of spiraling stairs, resting his hand on the railing.

"You'll find a bed. Get some sleep, my dear, and I'll see you in the morning," he says, stepping away, giving me a pat on the back.

I climb the unusual staircase. The landings range from being a few feet wide to others as narrow as a few inches. After seeing his house, I am now certain that without the chains holding this island in place, it would indeed float away.

I finally reach the top of the stairs, entering a large domed room. It is magnificent. A large telescope, about twenty five feet high, extends through an opening in the roof, pointing aimlessly at the majestic night sky. Large archways line the circumference of the room, offering three hundred and sixty degree views of the breathtaking vista. I can make out a small burlap sack stuffed with hay near an archway. That must be the bed he was referring to.

I walk over to an archway and rest my shoulder against its frame, staring out into the night, my head still spinning from our conversation. Two things in particular leave me unsettled. First, I learned that my mom's journey was never meant to end with her defeating the White Witch. She knew that her powers would be no match. Her journey, all along, was to help me. I am the only one who would stand a chance against her. Why me? How is it that Enkidu and my mom can have so much faith when I have so little?

And secondly, the White Witch has known since the attack on Garrett that I would be coming to face her, biding her time high up in the Mercurial Mountains, waiting for me, knowing I would not be able to rest without doing whatever I could to get my dad back. Am I playing into her hands? What other choice do I have?

Finding some temporary peace on the burlap sack, I close my eyes and drift off to sleep.

Sleep is the most amazing thing. Although I am awake, it feels so great to just lie here, the occasional breeze blowing across my face. I feel myself drifting back to sleep. I convince myself I have to go get up. Opening my eyes, I am surprised to see two more staring back at me. I scream and jump up.

"What are you doing up here?" I cry out, aiming my hand, ready to strike.

I am looking down at a sad and ugly looking creature. It has bulbous blue eyes with large floppy ears that dangle past its shoulders.

"Please don't harm me. I didn't mean to startle you!" it squeaks, raising its hands defensively. "I'm Sprigs. Enkidu sent me up here to inform you that breakfast is ready."

Feeling bad, I lower my hand. "I'm sorry, but I wasn't expecting to wake up with something staring at me!"

I notice that Sprigs is still cowering near the ground. I put the little guy back on his feet.

"Don't worry, I am not going to hurt you," I smile. "Let's go have breakfast."

Sprigs and I make our way down the stairwell towards a delicious smell coming from the kitchen. The stairs prove to be much more difficult to descend but I reach the ground floor with relief.

"Breakfast, you two!" Enkidu shouts from the kitchen. We take our seats as Enkidu emerges with a steaming plate piled high with meats, cheeses, and fruit. My stomach is growling.

"As long as it doesn't involve magic, I'm actually pretty good at things," he smirks, setting the plate on the table. To my surprise, it does indeed look delicious.

Few words are spoken between us as we devour the plate until nothing but crumbs remain. I am the one to speak first.

"Enkidu, who's this little fella? He gave me quite the scare this morning," I ask, as Sprigs's tennis ball sized eyes turn to look at me.

"Aw, him? He was a gift from your mother. I didn't like him at first. Very odd thing, but he's grown on me."

"Where did she find him?" I ask. Sprigs seems to be enjoying all the attention.

"When your mother found me, she stayed here, just as you are doing now. She knew her powers would need to be refined if she was to acquire for you more powerful Ais for your travels."

Enkidu drinks from his mug.

"She went to a sacred place, about a day's journey from here called Evermore. There, beneath the ruins, she found Sprigs and a powerful Ai named Kitsune," he continues, and reaches into his pocket, pulling out a gold wristlet and placing it on the table. He continues, "It's yours now".

I stare at the gold band and ask, "What makes this Ai so powerful?"

Enkidu lights up. "My child, it's not just Kitsune on its own; it's the fact that this Ai complements and completes the two you currently have."

"What do you mean?"

He continues, "The two Ais that you currently are wearing: Luna and Artemis, are both based in the elemental property of Light. You may have noticed that Artemis is best suited for offense. Luna, on the other hand, is best suited to providing your basic needs and utilities. Kitsune completes that circle — providing you with a range of defensive spells. Together, they form the Light Trifecta. These trifectas: Light, Earth, Fire, and so on, are the most powerful combination of Ais you can wear at one time."

I continue to stare at the gold band, hanging on every word that Enkidu says.

"And you, my darling..." he says, leaning in closer, "have the first known complete set! If you can learn to wield the collective power of these Ais, you just may stand a chance against the White Witch." Enkidu sinks back into his chair.

Feeling overwhelmed once again, I question, "And how am I supposed to learn that?"

Enkidu laughs out loud. "From me!"

I look up at the hole in the ceiling from yesterday. Here goes nothing.

Enkidu actually ends up being a much better teacher than he ever was in practice. I learn that he had used the cave beneath the floating island as a training ground for my mother before me, filling the cave with a bunch of deadly monsters which tested all of my abilities.

We practice going through the dungeon for the next three days: slaying waves of revolting spiders, and, my least favorite, cave lampreys, which wait for me in the dark shallow water. I have a close call with one of them as it shoots out of the water and begins to spiral itself around my body, its eyeless head inching its way toward my face. Luckily, Enkidu isn't far away and is surprisingly able to aim a clean shot at it.

The last obstacle in the dungeon is a creature to which Enkidu has given the name Gilgamesh. It can fly and is a mix between a bat and a large scaly lizard. Living its life in darkness, it can't see, and relies on its high-pitch screech to locate its enemies. It is no doubt the most challenging of all the creatures I have faced so far. Enkidu has him trained to cower at the sound of a whistle when things are getting too tough for me.

The more time that I spend in the dungeon with Enkidu, my confidence grows in my abilities. The Ais also grow in power with me, with Artemis's light arrows becoming so powerful we hesitate to continue using them for fear of the cave collapsing. Luna's light gains the ability to stun and temporarily blind creatures as I prepare to mount an attack. Kitsune proves to be irreplaceable, his light barriers saving me multiple times from vicious attacks.

On the last day, I stand once again in Gilgamesh's presence, dodging between stalagmites, avoiding an impact from his tail, which is covered in large poisonous spikes. Enkidu has allowed Gilgamesh to attack longer each time before he blows the whistle. Today it feels as if he'll never blow that stupid whistle. Gilgamesh swoops in, preparing to slam his tail in my exact position. I roll away just in time but not before one of the spikes grazes my side as I spin.

My side begins to burn in pain, and, without thinking, based on my new instincts, I send one of Artemis's light arrows into its gut as it flies overhead. In one instant, the cave is ignited in a brilliant white light. Pieces of Gilgamesh begin to rain down on Enkidu and me. The smell is horrendous.

Enkidu stands there, wiping his eyes clear of guts and blood. "Whelp, I think you're ready."

While Enkidu and I were training, Sprigs always had a warm meal ready for us at the end of the day. Tonight is no different. I have come to really appreciate him throughout my stay. I'll miss this little guy.

That night, Enkidu and I sit side by side, feet dangling over the edge of the island. It is a calming and tranquil moment. We stare up into the sky, observing the planetary ring of Mythe, and revel in its beauty. It floats high above us, like a moving river of shimmering diamonds cutting through the night sky, emitting luminous colors that seem to change when seen from different angles.

Enkidu leans over to me and says, "Do you see the glowing ruins in the distance? That is Evermore. That is your next stop."

I can clearly make them out ahead.

"It is about a day's journey from here. Evermore will be a safe sanctuary for you to take refuge in tomorrow night. It is where your mother found Kitsune and Sprigs. She has made it safe for you."

"How far from there is it to the mountains?" I ask.

"About another day, but listen closely. The desert beyond Evermore is much more treacherous. There you will undoubtedly face some of your greatest challenges. It is filled with sand worms who circle the mountains, drawn to their radiating power. There is one particular monster you must avoid at all costs: the king of the desert. He goes by the name Lazarus. He will show you no mercy."

The image of the passageway that Syd and I stumbled upon appears in my head. It terrifies me to think that he is out there somewhere.

"The sand worms are drawn to noise and sudden movements. Do whatever you can to tread lightly once you pass Evermore."

We sit there for a few more minutes, allowing me time to absorb what lies ahead. I feel a soft tap on my back and hear Sprig's voice, "Your beds are made and ready for your retirement!"

"Thanks, Sprigs. We'll be in shortly," I reply.

Sprigs remains standing there, and says, "I'm going to miss you. Good luck on your journey." He gives me a hug and looks up. "I know you can do it." He holds on a bit more and then trots off back to the house.

When Sprigs is out of earshot, Enkidu adds, "Phoenix, one last thing. I have been observing the White Witch intensely for quite some time now. I know what she plans to do. Should you not succeed, she will mount an assault upon all of Mythe. She wishes to use you as her greatest weapon. If that were to happen, all would be lost. Please, do not fail."

CHAPTER FIVE
AND SO IT BEGINS

The next morning I say my final goodbyes to Enkidu and Sprigs. It is hard to let go, knowing that I may never see them again. Sprigs has packed my bag full of supplies for my two-day journey. Even though I didn't spend too much time with them, we all grew very close. With my face to the wind, I begin trekking through the desert sands.

The floating island becomes smaller and smaller before it is swallowed by the dunes. I do have to admit that it would have been a very lonely journey without the company of my Ais. Kitsune is a welcome addition to our party. His demeanor is unlike Artemis or Luna. He has a deep calming voice and an astute understanding of our situation. It is an interesting day, to say the least. As I make my way to Evermore, I encounter a bevy of different living things, most notably vicious sand sharks, disgusting beetles, and large repulsive desert crabs. Without my training, there would have been no chance at making it here.

It was just a few hours ago that I arrived at Evermore. The suns were setting and casting their final light upon the ruins. It was a surreal moment, walking between towering pyramids and large stone structures obviously abandoned long ago. As night fell, the structures began emitting a soft cerulean glow, like what I saw for the first time from Enkidu's island. The only sound breaking the unnatural silence were my gentle steps through the sand.

I came across no troubles, as Enkidu promised. I felt my mom's protection as I made my way to a large pyramid at the edge of the sanctuary. Grabbing the stones, I climbed higher and higher until I reached the top.

I now find myself sitting here in the night. My hair flows in the warm breeze as I am bathed by the light of Mythe's ring and the pale glow of the pyramid. My vantage point beholds an awe inspiring sight. The Mercurial Mountains majestically rise out of the sands, reaching towards the sky, their peaks radiating soft green beams of light that seem to dance high above them.

At their base, I see them. The sand looks alive, twisting and churning. Some breach like giant whales coming up for air, while more still can be seen moving beneath the surface. I ask myself, how can one place be so beautiful and yet so terrifying at the same time?

CHAPTER SIX
SAND WORMS

The mountains loom in the distance, getting closer with each step I take. Today it is taking a lot longer, as I have to be mindful of my every move. I struggle not to let my paranoia get the best of me. A few times I almost panic when I swear I could feel the sand move beneath me. The pressure of this constant state of stress and foreboding is taking its toll on me.

"You need a break, Phoenix," Kitsune suggests. "See that large boulder up ahead? Let's stop there for a few minutes."

I don't argue and slowly make my way there. The boulder is quite large and it will be a short climb up to the top. The face is quite rough with grooves and ledges that I am able to use to hoist myself up. Sweating profusely, I am near the top when I lose my footing and fall to the sand below. Terror consumes me.

The ground quakes and I scramble to climb back up the boulder. I try to climb before the worms reach me. It will only be seconds, now.

Nearing the top again, my fingers wrap around the edge of the base block. Swinging my left hand up, I grasp the ledge. Pulling myself over it, I look back in time to see the first worm burst from the sand. Wriggling and swaying, it remains with half its body below the surface and half above.

I notice it has no eyes and large protruding tusk-like teeth. Scanning my surroundings, I notice a small rock to my left. Reaching out, and careful not to move any other parts of my body, I slide my hand over and lift the rock. I throw it into the desert. A soft thud is the only sound it makes but it is enough to distract the monster. Turning, the worm shoots at the spot and dives back into the sand. I take the opportunity to continue scaling the rock, lifting myself over another ledge. I am only a few more feet away from the top when two more worms emerge.

Rolling to my back, I see one is already lunging at me. I dive to the side and roll away from it. The second attacks with a maw full of never-ending teeth. Knowing I don't have time to avoid it, I point and shoot an arrow of light into its mouth. It makes contact, severing a part of its head from its body. Not bothering to look back, I run to the final ledge and pull myself up to the top.

All three worms surround the boulder and continue their hunt, including the worm with half a head. It lunges again but I am able to block it with one of Kitsune's light shields. Their attacks are too frequent and too fast for me — not allowing any time to go on the offensive. Lunge after lunge, they begin to weaken my shield, the force pushing me backwards along the rock. Kitsune's energy is draining fast and it won't last for much longer.

And then it happens. A sonic boom explodes behind me, knocking out my shield, followed by a gale of wind that nearly blows me off the boulder's edge. A great winged beast plunges from the sky towards the injured sand worm, taking it in its beak. The worm's body snaps in half as the winged animal's jaw clamps shut, the bloody stump falling to the ground below.

The other worms immediately retreat, burying themselves beneath the sand, no doubt trying to escape the winged beast. I take cover as I hear the sound of its second approach. I hold onto the rock as tightly as I can as it flies overhead, followed by another powerful gust of wind. I have never seen anything so colossal move through the air so fast. It extends its talons and dives into the dunes, emerging with both worms, one in each of its enormous claws, gracefully flying away towards the mountains. I watch until I can see it no more.

"That..." Luna says in disbelief, "...was the most terrifying thing I have ever seen."

It takes us a while to recover from the shock of the events just past, but I know we are close now — the mountains tower above us.

The suns are beginning to sink below the horizon as we carefully tread our way closer to the mountain's gate. I can see it from here. Two soaring rocks jut from the ground, framing a dark passageway leading deep into the mountains. My eyes stare, fixed on the daunting entrance.

Closer and closer I approach, my concentration broken suddenly by Kitsune shouting, "Phoenix! We're being hunted! Look to your left!"

I look and see a dark shadow in the sky, growing larger as it moves fast, directly towards me. I recognize it immediately. It is one of the colossal winged beasts that attacked the sand worms earlier on the boulder. Except this time there are no sand worms — only me. I am its prey.

I break out into a sprint, running as fast as I can to the mountain's entrance. I know that is my only hope of survival, but it doesn't take long to realize — I will never make it in time. I am still at least a hundred yards from the opening. The animal is swiftly closing in.

The ground jolts beneath me, shooting me forward to land face first into the sand. The shaking intensifies. I look back to see a giant swirling vortex has appeared as if a plug has just been pulled from underneath the sand. And in that moment, emerging out of the center of the vortex, he appears. Shooting into the sky, Lazarus lunges upward. The winged beast has no time to react as it is swallowed whole right before my eyes. Lazarus falls back to the ground, releasing a massive explosion of energy and sand, tossing me uncontrollably into the air. I crash back into the ground.

"No..." Artemis says in astonishment, "... that ...was the most terrifying thing I have ever seen."

CHAPTER SEVEN
THE WHITE WITCH

Dazed from the shockwave of Lazarus's impact, I begin to regain my senses.

"We made it," sighs Kitsune.

Lifting my head, I watch the dust settling through fading sunlight and realize how far I was thrown in the chaos. The gate to the Mercurial Mountains rises above me.

The way in is wide and long, the mountains gradually rising up to define a path. It curves left and right. Shadow replaces sunlight. Threatening clouds replace blue sky.

The sand beneath my feet turns to rock as I enter. The rock is strange. It is darker, like a slate or obsidian. I can see my distorted reflection looking back me. The wind howls as it snakes up the mountain pass. I continue, darkness gradually swallowing me.

"Luna, some light, please," I ask, and, she fulfills my request.

Her light illuminates six tall statues lining my way on each side. Elaborate circular stone headdresses make the rest of their bodies seem thin and snakelike, their arms forming an X across their chests. As I get closer I recognize them to be the golems which attacked Garrett. It looks as if they have been carved into the stone as a way to intimidate anyone daring to enter.

"I don't like them!" Luna cries.

I remember it was the stone golems which took her mortal life. I comfort her, saying, "They are just statues. They can't..." Staring up at their faces, my phrase is cut short.

The eyes on all the golems come alive, glowing a fiery, ruby red. In unison, their heads turn to face us, causing rubble to plummet toward the ground. I take a step back in fear as I watch them uncross their arms and tear away from the wall, creating an avalanche of stone and rock.

I begin my assault, shooting intense spheres of explosive light, simultaneously erupting into a series of deafening blasts comprised of sound and light. I stumble backwards, keeping my eyes in their direction, looking for any signs of movement.

Pairs of red eyes emerge from the smoke. The golems are unscathed.

"Artemis! Let's give it everything we have!" I shout.

Artemis's necklace begins to burn around my neck, as I am drawing her energy into my hands. A hot orb begins to form between my palms, growing in size as I extend my hands outward. Bolts of energy shoot out at random intervals, striking everything around me. My hands, struggling to contain the power, begin to shake uncontrollably. With all the strength I have left, I cast the ball of energy and fire at the oncoming golems. It hits its mark, detonating into the most unbelievable display of piercing light and flame. Its seismic wave slams into me, sending me flying backwards.

I lie there taking in deep breaths, waiting for the smoke to disperse, my chest rising and falling. The outline of a golem becomes visible through the smoke, making its way towards me.

"I'm sorry, Phoenix." Artemis begins to cry. "I wasn't strong enough to save you."

I am paralyzed by fear as the stone hand wraps around me, drawing me up to its expressionless face. The last thing I remember before losing consciousness is staring into a pair of blazing red eyes, before being hurled into the jagged stone wall.

Waking, I can taste blood in my mouth. My head is throbbing and feels as if it's about to split open. The wailing wind rushes over me. I can feel my hair whipping across my face. My body aches and feels broken.

I can hear footsteps slowly approaching from behind, a sinister laughter accompanying it. I attempt to talk Kitsune but there is no response. I can't feel a connection with any of them.

"Well, well, well..." a voice sounds, "We meet again".

Her voice spills over me like icy water.

"Stand up and face me," I hear, as an invisible force lifts me off the ground and drops me to my feet. I cannot support my own weight and collapse onto the floor. She breaks out in laughter.

"I have been waiting for 12 years... for this?" She demands again, "Stand up and face me!" I feel the invisible force again this time yanking me up and holding me firmly in place. I am bound by what feels like tight ropes.

"That's better," she says. My vision is blurry but I can make out a glowing white figure approaching me. The hairs on my arms start to stand up as she draws nearer. I can feel the electricity in the air. I close my eyes. The tip of her cold finger caresses my face.

"You look so much like your mother," she spits.

I can feel the warmth of my anger begin to build up at the mention of my mom. She continues to circle me.

"Tell me, what does it feel like knowing you're about to die?" she jeers at me, inches from my face.

"You could always ask your husband," I retaliate.

I brace myself in anticipation of her reaction. But none comes. Instead, there is a long pause. My breathing quickens. I slowly begin to peer out, my vision clearing, finding myself staring into the white void of her eyes. A sickening smile spreads across her face.

"Why don't you ask him yourself?" she retorts. Her hand reaches under my chin and turns my head. I can see a person in the distance, restrained, struggling to free himself. It's my dad.

"Papa!" I shout, pushing against my invisible bindings. "Let him go!"

She snaps her fingers and my dad shouts, "Amy! Don't do this!"

Amy? Why would my dad shout my mom's name? Following my father's gaze, I stare upon the White Witch. My head spins.

"Don't do what? Kill our daughter?" she laughs. "After what you did to my brother? Do you really think I'd forgive you for condemning his soul to be tortured for eternity?"

My world crumbles around me.

"Lazarus wanted me to save you! I did everything that I could to protect him!"

"LIAR!" she screams, darting to my dad. She grabs his throat and his face starts to turn blue.

"You could have saved him, but instead you let him suffer. You could have stopped Prefect Gray in that auditorium. You chose not to. And now you will suffer like we have." She releases her grasp, my dad gasping for breath. She refocuses her attention on me. "You will watch her die."

"Phoenix!" my dad struggles to shout. She snaps her fingers again, muffling the last syllable of my name.

Anger rages inside of me. How could this be possible? This can't be true. I don't understand. She drifts towards me.

"How... how...why? Zuri?" I stutter. This can't be my mom.

"Zuri?" she dismisses. "I killed her. She was no match for me."

Angry tears flow down my face.

"I have been waiting for this moment for many long years. Your father has never known the love of a family member. He could never understand the pain of losing someone so close. The longer I waited here, the more painful I knew your death would be. It's time for him to find out." I feel my constraints disappear.

"You won't be needing these," she says, lifting up a ring, bracelet, and necklace. I watch as she tosses them into the air, sending a bolt of electricity through them, making contact. My screams are overlaid with the cries of Artemis, Luna, and Kitsune. Fragments of burning metal rain down.

Hatred takes me.

"It's just you and me now. Mother versus daughter."

I turn to face her. "I have no mother."

I lunge forward. A power that I have never felt before erupts from inside me. We are consumed in a sphere of flashing light and smoke as we begin to duel on the summit of the Mercurial Mountains. I dodge in between bolts of electricity, firing shards of ice in the opposite direction. We continue to exchange blows, lighting up the night sky, dancing along the mountain's edge. She sends a pulsating ball of light towards the ground which explodes into a brilliant wave of sparking energy, knocking me back. I can smell my singed hair as I gasp for breath.

Her foot stomps on my chest, pinning me. I can feel some of my ribs crack under the pressure. Blood is pouring down my face.

"Enough. It's time to fulfill the only purpose of your pitiful life. To die."

She raises her hand for the final blow. In that instant, there is a flash of light and a clap of thunder as her spell collides with mine, deflecting hers into the cliffside. I can see her stretch her hand above my head. I know it's over. My body convulses as an electrical current radiates through me. As my eyes begin to close, I see a shadow pass over me. My body relaxes. This must be how it feels to die.

"Phoenix! Phoenix!" I hear, as my eyes flicker open.

"Thank god you're alive," a voice says. It's Enkidu.

"What happened? Where's my dad?" I attempt to stand, sending pain shooting through my body.

He places his hand gently on my shoulder. "No, no... lie down. You're hurt pretty badly," he says. "I wish I had gotten here sooner. I might have saved..." he trails off.

"Saved who? Enkidu, please tell me. What's going on?" I plead.

He hangs his head. "After you left I kept watch over you through my telescope. I felt liked I owed it to Amy to make sure you arrived safely. When I saw the golems carry you off, and I knew you were in trouble, I tried to get here as fast as I could..." He pauses, a tear escaping his eye. "I got here. I saw Zuri electrocuting you. But before I could intervene, I saw your dad running towards her." He starts to sob. "Phoenix, he saved your life."

I start to cry with him.

"He ran...He grabbed her...It happened all so fast. They both tumbled over the edge." He covers his face with his hands. Pain takes my heart's place. He hugs me, and we are weeping into each other's arms.

I pull away, looking into his eyes. "Enkidu, that wasn't Zuri."

"What do you mean it wasn't Zuri?"

"It was my mom. It was my mom all along."

His mouth drops in disbelief. "What? What are you saying, Phoenix?"

"It was Amy! She was the one that killed Zuri." I pause. "She was the one that killed my dad."

The journey down the mountains was made in silence. We both attempt to piece together how it all happened. Enkidu and I grab each other's hands, trying to find reason amongst madness.

EPILOGUE

We stand over my dad's grave. Enkidu, Sprigs and I. A solitary tombstone rises over the tall blowing grass near Enkidu's home, our tears glistening in the light of the setting suns.

We found his broken body on our descent. No sign of my mother.

"What do you think happened to her?" I quietly ask Enkidu.

He sighs, "No doubt, she will reunite with her brother. As to what happens next, I am not sure."

I gaze out over the scene before me, taking a long deep breath, contemplating my next words.

"We have to find her."

He turns to look at me with a tender smile. "Of course we do."

I lay a rainbow colored flower on the headstone. We make our way down to the sands below where Enkidu has a hover bike waiting for us. He climbs on and hoists me up, with Sprigs on my back. I wrap my hands around Enkidu's waist as the engine roars to life.

It is in that resolute moment that Enkidu and I have an unspoken understanding. In spite of everything, in spite of all the terrible things that have occurred and the unknown journey ahead, in spite of meeting my mother again, which I know will come, that we are in this together.

See you back in Mythe soon.

The journey through Mythe continues
in our forthcoming game based on this book.

apixal.com
facebook.com/apixal
twitter.com/apixal
instagram.com/apixalgames

ACKNOWLEDGEMENTS

OUR 859 KICKSTARTER BACKERS
Without you none of this would have been possible.

OUR DEAR FRIENDS AND FAMILY
You've allowed us to dream and dare, never wavering your support.

BETA READERS
For reading this book in its early stages and giving us fantastic feedback that helped shape the final product.

JENS & PER KIILSTOFTE
The two best Sound Designers and Composers we could ever have decided to work with.

GARETH DAVIES
Thank you for bringing this book to life through your amazing artwork and illustrations.

AUDREY VAN RYN
Without you this book would be filled with many more grammar and punctuation issues.

LYNNE TORREY
Giving us the opportunity to work with young creative minds from your school.

ANNA NORMAND, XAVIER LAYTON, MICHAEL GRIECO, JACK MOORE, ANNA ABESADZE AND HANNAH BELDOTTI
Your amazing creature concepts for the Orbie, Valkyrie, Bakyll, and Fire Fairy.

PHIL MITOTES & MEGAN AUGUST
For giving us a very warm welcome to the local Cheyenne business community.

ABOUT US

ABOUT APIXAL

Apixal is a developer and publisher of entertainment software and literature. Founded in 2014, we are a young creative startup based in Cheyenne, Wyoming. Our passionate team, mainly made up of family members, are focused on creating well-designed, highly enjoyable entertainment experiences that excite and tease the imagination.

In September 2014, apixal launched a successful Kickstarter for Phoenix Dawn and the Rise of the Witch. The game is currently in production.

ABOUT ERIC TROWBRIDGE, FOUNDER & AUTHOR

Eric Trowbridge is the founder of apixal and leads business operations and art direction.

Before founding apixal, Eric worked for Apple from 2006 to 2014 leading retail teams in Los Angeles, New York City and Chicago. Previous to his work at Apple, Eric was the art director for various small budget and independent films. Eric spent time at both the Academy of Art University in San Francisco and the Los Angeles Film School studying art direction and computer graphics.

Eric was born and raised in Cheyenne, Wyoming and currently lives there with his two cats Hoover and Kennedy and his french bulldog Margaret.

ABOUT JOSH WALKER, AUTHOR

Josh is the Creative Story Director and oversees writing the Phoenix Dawn novels and story elements for the game. Josh is a published author with his first book series Luke Coles and has collaborated on other anthologies.

Josh can be found on his off time playing with his two kids, Sasa and Cloud (named after the Final Fantasy 7 character) and spending time with his wife Maca.

ABOUT HAYLEY RUIZ, CONTRIBUTOR

Hayley is the Creature Concept Designer and works in 3D modeling and animation.

Outside of apixal, she is a certified personal trainer and a passionate animal lover. She cares for 4 dogs, 2 guinea pigs and 2 birds. Her next animal will be a pig.

ABOUT JOSE RUIZ, CONTRIBUTOR

Jose is the Game Engineer focusing on textures, animation and particle systems.

Prior to joining apixal, Jose worked for the local police department and left in May 2015 to join the apixal team full time.

Outside of his duties at apixal, you can find him building and designing arcade machines in his basement.

ABOUT GARETH DAVIES, ILLUSTRATOR

Gareth is the Artist & Illustrator for the Phoenix Dawn and the Rise of the Witch novel. Gareth has a passion for everything design, games and Kettle Bell. He studied Architecture at the University of Bath and proceeded to follow his passions by choosing a career in game and entertainment design. He has extensive experience in illustration and animation work which can be viewed on his Instagram profile: instagram.com/spudonkey

He currently works in house for a game developer working on unannounced titles and is currently playing The Witcher 3 when he's not not doodling, working or reading.

IN LOVING MEMORIAM

Gunther & Roosevelt